IN SKATES TROUBLE

A CHICAGO REBELS NOVELLA

KATE MEADER

This novella is a work of fiction. Any references to historical events, real people, or real places are used fictitiously. Other names, characters, places, and events are products of the author's imagination, and any resemblance to actual events or places or persons, living or dead, is entirely coincidental.

Copyright © 2017 by Kate Meader

Cover copyright © 2017 by Sweet n' Spicy Designs

ISBN: 978-0-9985178-6-5

All rights reserved.

No part of this book may be reproduced in any form or by any electronic or mechanical means, including information storage and retrieval systems, without written permission from the author, except for the use of brief quotations in a book review.

To Marion
I'm so glad you found me

1

UP UNTIL ABOUT ten minutes ago, Ford Callaghan would never have dreamed of eavesdropping on a private conversation. True, his grandmother was known to leave a room telling people to argue loudly so she didn't have to strain herself, but she was from the trashier side of the family, and Ford's mom had raised him better than that. However, all bets were off when the conversation was about oral sex.

Or, more particularly, how the entire male species knew jack about it.

Only when he rolled his shoulders and discovered he was so flat against the back of the balcony sofa he could've melted into it did he realize that maybe he had more of Granny Tate in him after all. Something else struck him too: he had an opportunity not usually afforded to men. Didn't he owe it to his tribe to learn where every man had supposedly been going wrong?

"He called himself a cunning linguist," one of the women said, her voice carrying clearly from the adjoining hotel room balcony. "With a straight face."

Her balcony mates—two of 'em—let loose with sympathy chuckles.

"At least he knew the terminology. When I suggested the stockbroker take a visit downtown, he looked at me like I was speaking a foreign language."

"So not cunnilingual, then?"

"Barely monolingual." There was something familiar about this woman's voice. Girlish and musical, like Marilyn Monroe. "What about you, Addy?"

Ford perked up at the mention of that name. *Addy.* For the last ten minutes, hers was the voice of the three women that pleasurably twisted his insides. Quieter than the others, she spoke with a smoky rasp. He didn't recognize it like he did Marilyn's, but something within him sensed an affinity.

"My ex would need a GPS to find a clit. And knowing him, he'd argue that the directions were all wrong anyway because they were given in a woman's voice."

Their laughter covered Ford's own low chuckle of appreciation.

"But there's nothing better than a guy who's not afraid to get down in the trenches," Addy continued. "Who eats you out like he plans to put it on his résumé as a marketable skill."

Ford shifted in his seat, carnal warmth flushing his veins at her plain speaking. He wondered what she looked like. He had it in his head she was a dusky-eyed brunette with lush waves falling over her shoulders, long enough to reach the rosy tips of her full, high breasts. That hair would brush against his chest as she prowled down his body, demonstrating her own marketable skills—

He raised his soda to his lips and took a sip to cool the hell down.

The conversation was continuing as if that brief visit to Ford's Fantasy Land had never occurred. *Kinda rude, ladies.*

"Addy, we're going to have to get you back out there. You're thirty-two, but you act like you're ninety-two. Guilt-free orgasms, that's what you need."

So, six years older than Ford, not some *Girls Gone Wild* coed. He liked that. And that get-you-back-out-there comment was the kind of thing said to a woman who'd been out of the game for a while. Maybe the ex with the X-marks-the-clit aversion had done a number on her. Or maybe she'd been wasting her time on men who couldn't appreciate her.

If Ford was sure of one thing, it was that a woman like this would find untold levels of appreciation in his bed.

Mental headshake. As the star right winger with the Cup-winning New Orleans Cajun Rajuns, Ford wasn't exactly hurting for female company. Four weeks ago, they'd pulled it out by winning the final game of the series against the New York Spartans. That night he was drowning in offers to keep those good times rolling, but he'd decided against going for a swim. At twenty-six, he was a bit young to be hanging up his condoms, yet the idea of another meaning-less fuck with another meaningless puck bunny held little appeal.

Doing the Cup tour in his hometown of Chicago, he'd thought it might clarify his thinking. Something was miss-ing. He ached for—shit, he didn't know what. A connection, which sounded pretty freakin' sappy. The day after tomor-row, Ford would take the Cup to visit his junior club, the youth hockey team of the Chicago Rebels, one of the two big franchises in the city. Rebels fans might be bitter about not even making it to the division playoffs, but Ford still got plenty of love from his hometown despite hanging his skates in New Orleans.

"I know, I know," Addy murmured. Yep, they were on a first-name basis now. "Every guy takes one look and immediately makes up his mind. I just want to meet someone without all the games and preconceptions."

"That's why you should come to my dinner party tomorrow. I have just the guy," said the woman with the familiar voice. It really niggled that he couldn't place it.

Addy groaned, and though Ford knew it was a groan of frustration, all he could hear in it was pleasure. Specifically, the pleasure he'd provide her, given the opportunity.

"The bean counter?" Addy asked. "Tell me, is a combover involved?"

More laughter, then: "I'd never do that to you. It's more of a . . . creative Mohawk."

This sent them all into raucous hoots that were cut short when the Marilyn sound-alike commented that it was late and she had a young stud waiting for her at home. Sarcasm noted. Two minutes later, the party had broken up and the balcony was quiet again.

Disappointment settled over him like a rain-weighted cloud. Those flash reveals of the lady psyche hadn't satisfied his erotic curiosity or nudged him any closer to figuring out what women wanted. Or what Addy wanted . . . beyond an enthusiastic tongue. Was she staying in the room next door —and would she be willing to educate a clueless jock on the finer points of the female orgasm?

Oh, the places your dirty mind will go, Killer.

Smiling ruefully at his idiocy, he checked his phone, remembering now that he had turned it off completely as soon as the locker-room conversation next door had turned shockingly intimate. That said it all right there, didn't it? Not wanting to risk even the lowest vibratory buzz, he'd made a

In Skates Trouble 5

conscious decision to remain hidden in the shadows like a creeper. Nice.

A text from his brother Jackson: *Marcy wants to know if lasagna is okay for dinner on Friday.*

Familiar threads of guilt panged his chest. He would be staying with his brother and his family in Bridgeport on Chicago's South Side the day after tomorrow. What he hadn't told them—what he hadn't told anyone—was that he'd arrived in town a couple days early. He wanted to hit Paulie's grave without his brother's recriminatory glances or the media latching on to the story of the Callaghan boys, all destined for greatness until it turned to shit one rainy night on I-90.

Plenty of time to feel like crap in the bosom of his family.

He turned the phone over on the side table, unbidden thoughts of the sultry-voiced goddess ensuring his wicked hard-on still raged. Christ, he hadn't sported that much wood in forever. The woman's voice had done that. Addy's voice.

What would she say if he knocked on her door— assuming it *was* her door?

What would *he* say?

I couldn't help overhearing your conversation and how you're looking for a guy who won't play games. Who knows his way around a woman's body. Can tongue-fuck all night long. Bonus: a full head of glorious hair, no creative Mohawks here. A veritable salad.

Yeah, that'd go over well. *You're an idiot, Callaghan.*

He stood, the throb in his dick lessening as the reality of the situation crowded out his fantasy. Nice while it lasted. Resigned to a lonely night with his right hand and the memory of his neighbor's voice for company, he gripped the balcony door and slid it back.

A husky sound echoed in the still of the night, so quiet that for a moment he imagined it was in his head.

"Leaving so soon, Mr. Eavesdropper?"

2

THAT SHARP INTAKE of breath Addison Williams heard from her neighbor was enormously gratifying. *Gotcha, mister.* He clearly had no idea she'd been there for the last five minutes after the girls left—nor that she'd been acutely aware of his presence for the fifteen before that.

She swore she heard him swallow before he spoke. So. Damn. Cute.

"I could say I didn't intend to listen in, but it'd be a brass-balls lie."

"Good. I hate liars."

"What's your opinion on eavesdroppers?"

Smiling, she let the moment ride for a few extra beats. "Not my favorites, either, but more understandable. It's human nature to be curious."

"All hail human nature."

He still hadn't moved from the sliding door, and no illumination filtered from the room. The Chicago city lights cast a fuzzy, indistinct glow over the hotel's façade, but at fifteen floors up, that glow didn't quite reach the balconies. She had a sense of him being big, over six feet, which a woman of her particular height always appreciated in a man.

When she remained silent, he spoke again. "In this case, I'd say it was a good thing I was listening in. Doing a service, really."

"A service for me?"

"A service for humanity. Well, first for men, but women would ultimately benefit."

Leaning back on the balcony's sofa, Addison considered the next move. Why was she talking to this stranger again? She suspected neither Liz nor Harper had even realized he was there, hovering in the shadows, absorbing the slightly raunchy back-and-forth. Was that why she'd been so unusually vocal about her ex-husband's failure to please her in bed? Was she issuing a challenge to this man, to any man listening?

I'm a woman and I have needs, dammit.

That sounded silly, silly enough to make her chuckle.

"What's so funny?" Softly spoken. Genuinely curious.

She couldn't say what she was really thinking—what woman ever could?—so she fell back on responding to his earlier statement. "The idea that any man would perform a service for humanity. From my experience, men are mostly selfish."

He tutted. "So cynical. And you haven't seen me in action."

"A doer, not a talker, are you?"

"No reason I can't be both, Addy."

Her breath caught at his use of her name. How did he know she was the one who'd remained behind? Had he been listening that closely?

"Your voice stood out in the group," he murmured,

offering an explanation she hadn't sought aloud. "You have a voice like syrup, Addy."

The way he said that turned *her* to syrup. Warm, gooey, treacley waves that pumped slowly through her veins, heating her body in anticipation.

But, of what? Nothing could happen here. This was just a harmless flirtation she'd use later when she slipped between the zillion-thousand-thread-count sheets in her hotel room. She was in town to meet with the marketing team for her lingerie line and to prepare for her official move to Chicago in a few weeks. Right this minute, whispering secrets in the sensual dark, she had zero regrets at turning down Harper's offer to stay at her townhouse in Lake Forest, just north of the city.

She doubted Harper's guest room came with a whiskey-voiced stranger as a perk.

The stranger stepped away from the door, a couple feet closer to the side near her balcony. Panic made her skin itch. She didn't want that. If he saw her—the real her—the sexy vibe would be ruined.

"Could . . . could you stay back? In the shadows." The request sounded ridiculous on her tongue, and she immediately regretted it. He'd think her a total nutjob.

"Sure, Addy," he said, low, certain, his tone accepting in a way that made what she'd said not sound odd at all. "Okay if I sit for a while?"

"If you'd like."

Not just okay. Wanted. *Desired.*

But, why? Because . . . it had been a while since her nerve endings had fired in the presence of a man. Since her skin had felt tight and her belly wriggled with want.

Awareness of his size as he moved to the sofa at the other side of the balcony made her doubly conscious of her own body. He might be an actuary or a spy or a kitchen gadget salesman, but it didn't matter. Just as it didn't matter that she was Addison Williams, ex-wife of a powerful magnate who had wanted a trophy not a partner. She should have known that any man who calls a woman after he spots her in a Victoria's Secret catalog—and what was he doing with that catalog, she might ask?—was probably not interested in her scintillating conversation.

"So you were saying?" she asked the stranger next door.

"Was I?"

"About your services to humanity."

He chuckled, raspy and glorious, and it shot a direct line to a neglected spot between her legs.

"Right. My services." He paused, perhaps considering how to phrase what came next. "My bout of eavesdropping gave me precious insight into the female mind. I hate to think my people have been falling down on the job."

Cheeks heating, she laughed, remembering what she'd said. "Just their tongues. Although now you mention it, there have been a few droopers in the last couple of years."

"Droopers with you, Addy? Can't believe that. A dead man's dick would raise the lid of a coffin on hearing that voice of yours."

Oh, he was a smooth one. Yet, there was a boyish sincerity to him that scooped out a cavity in her chest. How old was he? He didn't sound as old as her ex, but he didn't sound too young either.

What the hell did it matter? It wasn't as if she would ever see him face to face. As if anything would happen here in shadow-sheltered safety.

"Reports of my dick-raising abilities have been vastly exaggerated." She might have lowered her voice to bedroom husky there. Just testing the waters.

"Like hearing that word out of your mouth, Addy."

"What? Exaggerated?"

"You say dick and mine gets hard."

She blinked at his provocative words, ones that left no doubt what they were both thinking. The honesty of it should have terrified her but instead, it toppled her. Time ticked, the air pressurized, an explosion waiting to happen.

"So, what are you in town for?" he asked, as if he hadn't just casually mentioned his erection to a complete stranger. One who had admittedly provoked him, but still. Sure, let's pretend *that* hadn't happened.

She had been silent too long. Without visual cues, all he had was her words to go on. In the thick and sultry late July air, his regret was palpable, and she wasn't sure if she was glad he'd backed off.

"I'm here on business."

"What kind of business are you in?"

"Fashion. Selling into department stores." Half-true, or at least that's where her career was now headed. Deciding on bravery, she added, "Lingerie. That's what I sell."

She could sense his (sexy) grin, even in the dark. For a moment, she wondered if she'd overplayed her hand, but his next statement told her she'd made the right call.

"What I said before about how your words affect me . . . I'm sorry if I came on too strong. I was just thinking about what you said earlier. No games."

That he'd remembered was either exceptionally creepy or extraordinarily evolved. She liked how he made her feel so she went with the latter. There was safety in the dark.

"You didn't go too far. Straight talk is a virtue. Dirty talk is a goddamn blessing."

So it was glib, a deliberate effort to lower the level of discourse and raise the stakes. His laugh was even more beautiful than his chuckle. Deep and resonant, making her breasts ache and her sex clench.

"Maybe that's what's been wrong with the fuckwits who need a map around your body, Addy. Maybe they need better directions."

Suddenly, her jeans felt too tight, and not only because the generous ass that paid her bills and got countless horny teenagers and their fathers off was filling it a little too well. No, they felt like a fetter on the bloom between her legs. This was usually a male problem with the erections they could barely contain, but damn if her clit didn't feel positively Grinch-like: three times too big.

"Are you implying I hold some responsibility for my orgasms, Mr. Eavesdropper?"

"Believe me, Addy, guys do much better with their woman telling them what they need. They love hearing her give instructions, showing them where his fingers touching work best, directing them to the spot that needs my tongue on it now."

In the haze of his defense of all those poor misguided men who needed help, she almost missed it. That switch from the general to the particular. From the actions of all men to the action of one—the one who right this second was turning her on like a lamp.

My tongue, he'd said.

She bit down on her lip to throttle the moan aching to find its voice. He needed to be quiet now. If he said one more word, she'd have her hand down her jeans before she could say "*Wanna come over and do me, Eavesdropper?*"

A wayward hand found its way to her breast. Just a light glance to ease the ache.

"You touching yourself yet, Addy?"

Holy shit, way to crank it up, stranger.

In Skates Trouble

She dropped that hand like it had burned her sensitive, forbidden flesh. Caught in this no-man's land of pleasure and torment, unsure how to proceed, she shook her head. Because, of course, he could see *that*.

"Addy, sweetheart, you okay over there?"

"Fine," she squeaked.

Another low chuckle, but this one sounded as pained as it did sexy.

"You lying to me, Addy?"

"Um..."

"No games, sweetheart. Straight talk is a virtue, remember?"

But only about things that didn't matter. She'd tried honesty with her ex and it had wrenched them apart instead of bringing them closer. *I need my career. I need to be someone other than a wife.*

In this moment, she could be forthright about this. About her needs. Honesty would give her power.

"I—I'm not okay," she managed. "I'm aching."

His indrawn breath turned to a heartfelt groan that echoed in this world-away-from-it-all bubble.

"Addy, you're killin' me." She could hear his shallow breaths and she wondered how warm they'd feel on her bare skin. Mostly, she wondered about his hands. She liked big hands. Blunt, coarse palms that would cover her ample ass—because even a woman with a booty that made her fortune appreciated hands that made it look smaller.

"I want you to tell me what you want, how you like it." He was struggling to speak, each word fighting to find air. Fighting to find her. "I want you to imagine I'm over there, kneeling between your thighs, waiting for instructions."

Instructions. Straight talk. Taking responsibility for her orgasms.

She was in charge here, as her imaginary, yet shockingly real lover bowed before her, ready to serve. How would he use those big hands? Would he be slow in moving from her ankles up her calves and finally between her thighs, every inch gained a mile taken from her resistance?

She didn't know what to do next. She knew what she wanted to do, but could she?

You'll never see him again. You'll never see him at all. Just listen to that voice and let him listen to you.

Listening . . . that's all she'd ever wanted.

The hiss of her jeans zipper was louder than she expected, probably because it was the sound of no return.

"Good girl. Make sure there's room for me. For my greedy mouth. All the way down. Now, what should I do next?"

Take off your pants. Take your cock in your hands and stroke it from thick base to shining tip.

"Addy?"

Oh, God, she was doing this. They were doing this.

"Um—take my panties off? They're silky—"

"What color?"

"Cream. It's my favorite color. It looks good against my skin." She shoved her jeans to mid-thigh, the rough jerk taking her panties so they lay half-on, half-off.

Poor, confused panties.

"I love this part," he said, his voice rasping barely above a whisper. "When I catch that first glimpse of you. Are you bare or do you keep yourself warm with a little strip?"

She smiled at his turn of phrase. "Not completely bare." After years on the modeling circuit, she'd gone back to nature—or nature with a landscaped trim. She pushed both her panties and jeans down and kicked them both off with

In Skates Trouble

15

her heels. The soft thud made it clear that clothes removal was in progress.

Sanity removal wasn't far behind.

She was naked from the waist down on the darkened balcony of a downtown Chicago hotel, because a stranger had urged her on.

This was fucking crazy.

Then she heard it, a scraping sound from his side. He was unzipping, too.

Even among the cavalcade of emotions hurtling through her veins, she was able to pluck out the one that signified relief. She wasn't alone in this madness. They were a team— a horny, reckless, fuck-it team.

"Now, Addy, what would you like me to do next?"

Inhaling a ragged breath, she moved tentative fingers to her thigh. If she'd thought removing her panties was one step toward the ledge, this next one would hurtle her over into the abyss.

"I want your—" The words refused to form.

"What, sweetheart?"

"I want—" *Nope, can't do it.*

"Tell me what you need, Addy. Tell me what I can give you."

His generosity sealed her fate. "I . . . I need your fingers to part me. To stroke softly."

He hummed, deep in his throat, and that sound did something to her. Something wicked and wanton, and oh so wild.

"How will I find you?"

Say it say it say it. "Wet."

And she was. Oh, God, the sparks that flew through her on that first contact lit up her sex-starved body. No man should have this much power. She'd spent two years recovering from a man who'd exercised terrifying control over her.

She shook her head, annoyed at her thoughts for going there. This was no power trip. The stranger didn't know a thing about her except that she had high standards for oral sex and that her voice apparently did things to him. And hell, if his voice didn't do something for her. Something she'd never experienced before.

Absolute abandon.

Accept this as your due. Enjoy what this one-time, never-to-be-repeated experience offers you.

"My mouth's watering, just thinking of how you taste, Addy. Give me a preview. Tell me how good you taste."

Did he mean that she should . . . do that? Needing a moment to wrap her head around this request, to just enjoy the pleasure of his voice urging her on, she continued to stroke. Each velvet swipe coiled her belly tighter. Eddies of pleasure swirled, ever-tautening, and she took care to avoid her clit. One touch and she'd shoot off so fast it would embarrass them both.

Was he touching himself, too?

"Addy," he moaned, and she listened for noises of—there it was. That muffled sound of soft/hard tugs. He was jerking off, and just that confirmation, hiked her pleasure to untold levels.

"How do you taste, sweetheart? I need to know. Need to know so badly."

She raised her fingers to her mouth and swiped them across her lips, flicking her tongue out to taste herself. Could he see that? Hear her movements from core to mouth?

"I taste good," she murmured, surprising herself, because she did. She'd never done that before. The action thrilled her, fueling her boldness. "You're going to love it." *When your tongue glides between my legs and finds me wet for you, you're going to love it.*

She wished she could say that out loud but judging by his reaction, she may as well have. He swore roughly. *Score.*

"Bet you're pretty and pink, right, baby? Bet you're a work of art. Those beautiful folds swelling under my tongue, that tasty cream gushing into my mouth, that hot little clit throbbing in my mouth."

Oh, God, her fingers shoved between her legs, roughly, her need mindless and grasping. His tongue inside her, his mouth hungrily eating her out was all she could think about, and the lightest glance across her clit was enough to make her come madly on that sofa in the dark. There was no stopping her cries of pleasure, no stopping the waves of sensation, no stopping the need he had stirred in her.

On her descent, she slumped boneless and listened for him, her only regret that, as he shouted her name when he released, she didn't know his.

3

FORD PACED HIS HOTEL ROOM, the same mantra playing over and over in his head.

You're a fucking idiot.

Every now and then he changed it up with fool or moron or even asshole when he was feeling particularly vitriolic, but the bottom line was the same. He had let Addy go without any idea how to contact her.

That she'd wanted this should have put his mind at ease. After he had come with such force on the balcony he might have hit the John Hancock Center two miles out, they'd both sat there for a few minutes, recovering in the night's stillness. He'd wanted to give her the chance to make the next move, and in delaying, he'd scared her off.

Thanks, she had said, and then smaller, quieter, *Good night.*

It sounded a lot like goodbye.

His lust barely slaked, he could have gone all night. Shown her what every man she'd ever allowed in her bed had done wrong. They would have feasted on each other until dawn.

In Skates Trouble 19

Instead, he'd let her go and then spent the night alone, jerking himself raw to the memory of those sounds she'd made when she came. Filled with regret this morning, he'd gone out to the corridor to knock on her door only to find housekeeping cleaning up. A dropped fifty led to the discovery that she had checked out.

Addy. He knew her first name. He knew the sounds she made when she imagined his fingers and tongue inside her.

He knew he was royally fucked.

His phone rang, a call from Jax. *Back to reality we go*.

"Hey."

"Marcy said to call."

Shit, he'd never answered the text from his brother last night because he was otherwise occupied getting a gorgeous stranger off on an open-air balcony in the middle of downtown Chicago. You couldn't make this shit up.

Penthouse, check your mail.

"Tell her lasagna sounds amazing. I'm looking forward to a home-cooked meal."

"You need to get yourself a woman instead of banging all those fans on the road."

Ford snorted. They rarely spoke, but Jax had to know Ford was too serious about hockey to spend his spare time screwing anything that moves. Of all the Callaghan boys, Ford had been the most focused, hard-working, and driven. He didn't have Jax's brute force or Paulie's natural talent, and now he bore the heavy mantle of the Callaghans, the dreams of their ghosts.

"Having a regular woman's no guarantee of a home-cooked meal. Life on the road tends to put a damper on that."

"Wouldn't know," Jax said on an exhaled breath.

No, he wouldn't. His knee had a pin in it, so he'd missed his chance.

After two seconds of their customary awkward, Jax picked up the slack. "The kids are dying to see you. They can't wait to touch the Cup. Pretty proud of their uncle even if he did do it with the Raisins instead of a decent team like the Rebels."

The Raisins was the not-so-nice nickname given to the Rajuns. It used to bother him, but then he won the Cup, so fucking whatever.

"Sorry to inform you, bro, but the Rebels suck."

Jax sighed, relief in that sound to be on the safer ground of local sports and the inevitable disappointment that came with being a Rebels fan. "Yeah, the old man's still got a death grip on the reins. He's been driving the team into the ground for years."

It was a commonly held belief that Clifford Chase's dominion over the Chicago Rebels had done more bad than good. They used to show promise but former player and NHL Hall of Famer Chase didn't want to spend the money for decent skaters. His daughter was on tap to take over, but Ford—and just about everyone in the league—had their doubts about how a woman would fare in the cut-throat, testosterone-drenched world of professional hockey. It wasn't as if this was pansy-ass football.

An alarm went *boom* in his head, and he had to struggle to refocus on the conversation. The voice on the other end of the line was no longer his brother's.

"Uncle Ford?"

His nephew Coby, a wicked talented little skater who had all the makings of a great defensive linesman when he grew up. Give him twelve more years.

"Yeah, buddy, how's it hangin'?"

In Skates Trouble

"Are you going to bring me a Rajuns shirt signed by the players?"

Ford flicked a glance to his suitcase where he had packed away three Rajuns shirts, all autographed by the team. He'd even had to walk in on Kazakov's hairy ass as he celebrated with not one, not two, but three "fans" on the night of the final game. Everyone was scattering the day after, so he took one for the team and bleached his eyeballs later.

The things he did for his family.

"Don't worry, I've got you covered. Looking forward to seeing you. All of you."

That tinge of guilt reignited in Ford's chest. Surely Jax wouldn't be angry Ford played it this way, arriving in Chicago a couple days ahead of schedule. Coming in early had given him time to adjust to being back in his hometown after so long. Away games didn't count.

I've needed the quiet. The anonymity. Last night he'd reveled in guilt-free pleasure with a woman who knew nothing about his stats or his big contract or his tragic backstory.

The sound of a scuffle heralded the arrival of another nephew. Ford spent a few more minutes playing famous hockey-player uncle before he rang off.

Damn, he missed them. He missed them all. He didn't want to play famous, *absent,* hockey-player uncle forever. At the grand old age of twenty-six, it wasn't as if he'd been on the road forever, but the yearning to find a home—to *make a home*—was singeing the edges of his heart.

Now what was it that had pinged him while he was talking to Jax? He played back the conversation in his head. Chicago Rebels. Clifford Chase. Chase's daughter.

Harper.

He knew he'd recognized her voice, that melodious, fifties sex-kitten lilt. He'd met her a few times over the years, usually at some hockey PR event. If she were plain, she would've had a better shot at being accepted in the locker room. But she was far from plain. She was an attractive woman with cupid-bow lips and a sexuality she was unafraid to flaunt.

For all her multiple attractions, however, she had nothing on her friend.

Addy.

Ford smiled to himself. Guess he had a call to make.

4

ADDISON WAS USHERED into Harper's *oh-let's-just-call-it-a-mansion-shall-we* in Lake Forest, a wealthy water-fronting enclave just north of Chicago, by a woman dressed as French maid. This did not surprise her. Harper was known for her amazing parties and she always hired catering staff, but really, the French maid outfit was a tad much.

A long day meeting with the marketing team for her upcoming lingerie line had left Addison pooped. Relaxing in a hot, sudsy bath would be just the ticket, especially the claw-foot tub in the guest bathroom adjoining her temporary home for the next few days. Harper hadn't blinked when Addison said she'd take her up on her offer to stay after all. Getting out of the hotel after what happened last night was imperative.

The greeter must have been told to take jackets. As Addison wasn't wearing one, she merely flailed her hands and gestured to the salon. Yep, Harper called it "the salon" like she was Dorothy Freakin' Parker reincarnated.

"You can go right—"

"Addy!" Harper bounded out so quickly that Addison had to check the petite blonde's feet for skates. Her friend tossed sunny waves of hair over her shoulder and took Addison by the arm, gripping a little tighter than was comfortable. "A word, please."

"Everything okay?"

Harper bit down on her lip. "Yes . . . and no."

"Look, I'm really fine if the bean counter didn't show." She kept her voice in a whisper just in case he *had* shown and the news was worse than she feared. Such as he smelled like three-day-old cheese or sprayed saliva when he talked. "I'm not really in the mood to put on my first-date face."

Not after last night. Her mind strayed to the fantasy-made flesh. She yawned, still tired after she'd lain awake all night, her feet itching to race to her neighbor's room and see that initial orgasm to its logical conclusion: a hot-as-Hades stranger plunging into her over and over.

"That's not the problem," Harper went on, oblivious to Addison's sexy and very inappropriate daydreaming. "You see, we have another guest and well, he just showed up. I've met him a couple of times, so I couldn't really turn him away but . . ." She screwed up her face in a mix of embarrassment and disgust.

"But, what?"

"It's Killer Callaghan."

Killer who? Was that a WWF wrestler? Addison's blankness must have been reflected on her face.

"Ford Callaghan," Harper prompted, then lowered her voice to a conspiratorial whisper that wouldn't bounce off the marble-walled foyer. "Right winger for the Cajun Rage? The team that brought home the Cup a month ago? You know, your ex-husband's hockey franchise."

In Skates Trouble 25

Addison tried to recall a face, a body, a head of hair, but nothing came to her. The Rajuns' players all tended to blend together into one vast muscle mass. None of them had stood out during her three-year disaster-piece of a marriage, and if she had favored one with any attention, her ex would not have appreciated it. She'd always been a sports fan but after the split, with her ex taking hockey in the divorce, her interest had waned. Self-preservation had made that a necessity.

"Since the Great Escape, I haven't exactly been keeping tabs on the team's roster or their colorful nicknames. So there's a hockey player at the dinner table. Is he house-trained or should we expect juicy belches and ball-scratching?"

"I can probably go an hour before I need to be walked."

The ground yanked from beneath Addison's feet.

That voice.

It couldn't be, but she'd recognize it in . . . well, the dark. It was *him*, her hotel room neighbor, her dirty-talkin' fantasy man. How could he have known she'd be here?

No. It was a coincidence, nothing more. A crazy one-in-a-billion coincidence. He couldn't know she was the woman on that balcony, the woman who had turned into a wanton sexpot with very little encouragement. And he *wouldn't* know it was her.

Unless she spoke. A little late to be concerned about that because he must have already heard her speaking to Harper. What had he said about her voice? *A dead man's dick would raise the lid of a coffin on hearing that voice of yours.*

Oh. Shit.

Her heart jerked like a pinball around her body, her gaze following suit as she pivoted to meet the Panty Whisperer in the flesh. She had a sense of something big and blond and vaguely Viking pillaging her senses, and she quickly looked away as if that could make it all disappear.

Unfortunately the universe did not work this way.

She shot a look at Harper, trying to discern her friend's knowledge levels. Harper didn't give off smug or pleased, merely concerned.

Addison searched her brain for another explanation. Had he followed her? Was he a whacko nutjob after all?

Something clicked, locked, and knocked her on her ass.

This was the hockey player Harper had mentioned.

The one who had dropped by out of the blue for dinner.

The one who played for her ex-husband's team.

Double—no, triple—shit.

Unable to avoid reality any longer, she turned to where he stood at the entrance to the salon, though "stood" was all wrong. More like "loomed." She had underestimated his height. He was at least six feet four inches of brute strength, topped with shoulders as wide as a Buick, and further crowned with a head of dirty-blond hair that was a little on the long side. Plenty for her to hold on to.

Stop that!

"I don't think we've met," he said, all sexy-serious, and her body's reaction to that voice confirmed his lie. Her body knew that voice like a snake knew its charmer.

And worse—as if there was possibly another level to this cluster—his lie confirmed something else.

He knew who she was, even before she'd uttered a single word.

He was here. For *her.*

Her mind raced, making connections, dismissing theories, drawing conclusions. Was this planned? He knew her name. Had called it out when he came last night.

After he made her—*Oh, God.*

Apparently, he'd met Harper before and while Addison's friendship with the heir-in-waiting to the Rebels wasn't exactly Taylor Swift plus *insert current A-lister BBF here* levels of notoriety, it occasionally made the society pages on Addison's visits to Chicago. Primarily because she had a famous persona that pre-existed the connection to her ex-husband.

His boss.

"Miz Chayyyse!" A plaintive cry from the direction of the kitchen broke the tense silence.

"Never hire Bulgarians." Harper turned to the friendly neighborhood hockey player-stalker. "Ford, Addison. Addison, Ford. Ford, get Addison a drink, will you, while I see what the hell's happening to the food?" She click-clacked off, leaving them alone in the foyer.

They stared at each other while Addison tried to curb her racing pulse.

"What's going on here?" she asked, once sure she could speak without her voice cracking. She couldn't let him see that this was bothering her, or let anyone else present know they had history.

As of twenty-four hours ago.

"Last night," he started, moving forward, his voice low and dangerous and damn him, so sexy, "I swear I had no idea who you were. I came to find you this morning, and you'd already checked out. Then I was talking about the Rebels with my brother and I realized it was Harper's voice I'd recognized. I also remembered she'd said something about a dinner party, so here I am."

Such a simple explanation.

"Here you are? Just like that?" She rubbed her fingers against her chest, an old habit when she was feeling trapped. She'd practically rubbed a hole to her heart in the last year of her marriage to Michael.

"I wanted to see you again." He stepped in close, and God, his sheer size, and that sex-tinged voice in combination, made her knees melt. "I didn't set out to meet Addison Williams, famous model, ex-wife of Michael Babineaux, who also happens to be my boss."

Yes, those were all the niggling details, succinctly outlined in under one-hundred-forty characters. His strong brow creased above chocolate-brown eyes now darkened to an inky black. Was that anger? Frustration? Something else?

His reaction appeared genuine. He was as surprised as she to find out their true identities.

Fine. He was welcome to the benefit of her doubt. It shouldn't make any difference because she'd had no intention of meeting him outside of her fantasy. Just because she knew who he was did not change that. If anything, it made last night's decision to not take what happened any further especially prescient.

Of course, there was always the chance he wasn't interested in seeing her again now he had actually *seen* her. Up close, in the size-16 flesh. Not every man liked a woman with a little meat on her, and now that neither of them could use the darkness as an excuse, she'd understand if he wanted to back away slowly.

No number of magazine covers could eliminate those big-girl doubts.

As for her opinion of him? The guy was smokin'. In another lifetime, she'd totally tap that.

In the moments it was taking her to gather her wits, he had moved to within inches of her. Smooth outside of the shadows as well.

"I'm not sure what you're expecting here," she said,

increasingly overwhelmed by his presence as well as this situation. She was a large woman, and it took a helluva lot of man to make her feel like she could be picked up and put in his pocket.

"Just a nice dinner with a beautiful woman."

She refused to enjoy the wriggle of pleasure in her stomach. *He still wants me. Pathetic, you schizoid. You're gorgeous. Ten million Instagram followers agree.*

"Harper will be pleased you think so."

That amused him. "Electing to play coy? After all we've meant to each other, Addy?"

Her name on his lips was like gasoline to the fire in her blood. The Addison Williams of yesterday had not been coy. She'd been vocal, demanding, honest. But then it was safe in the dark.

"There won't be a repeat of last night," she affirmed, as much to herself as to him.

"You're right. I'm all about the variety. In the bedroom, in the foyer—or on the balcony." He grinned and *yowza, knock me over with the killer smile, why don't you*? "You look like you could do with a drink, Addy."

"Lead the freakin' way."

HARPER HAD ASSEMBLED an intimate crew of twelve for her dinner party: several Chicago power couples, an environmental activist, a novelist of some repute (big ego, low sales), and the Chicago Rebels lawyer, Kenneth Bailey, who hung on each of Harper's words like they were water to his thirst.

Then there was the hockey player and the accountant.

The bean counter's combover was less creative Mohawk and more wispy strands that wouldn't survive a gentle breeze intact. Swooping in from the back, angry, *frosted* tips stood to attention on the crown of his head. The style turned his forehead into a five-head. He was also shorter than her, by at least four inches.

How could Harper have possibly thought this guy might be a good match for her? Since Michael, Harper had tried to steer Addison to safer (read: boring) harbors. The women had become insta-friends one night, sitting in the owner's box during a Rebels-Rajuns game. While the WAGs of other team owners looked down on Addison's modeling career, Harper saw a business woman anxious to escape the bimbo image that inevitably plagued those who made a living wearing little or no clothing. After the divorce, Harper had been her biggest cheerleader as Addison reconstructed her life, reestablished her independence, and took tentative steps on her new path.

Out of respect for her friend, Addison would give Ben the Bean Counter a shot. She'd say one thing for him: he was very attentive, and not just to her cleavage as most men usually were when faced with Addison Williams, renowned full-figured lingerie model. (Please don't call her plus-sized.) Although, his lack of leering might be directly correlated to the lack of cleavage on display. She had elected to cover up with a silk shell so her "date" wouldn't get confused between her breasts and her face.

Meanwhile, her breasts were in a state of confusion all on their own. *Should we point toward Ford Callaghan's chest like hunk-seeking missiles? Or should we nipple-pop hard against this erotically thin fabric every time he casts a smoldering look in our direction?*

"So, Addison," Ben the Bean Counter started, "Harper tells me you're designing your own line of plus-sized lingerie. That sounds interesting."

"Don't think they say plus-sized anymore, dude," Ford said, catching her eye.

She scowled at him. *Stow your phony support, Callaghan. These big-girl panties are locked tight!*

"Oh, really?" Ben asked. "I didn't know we'd become that PC."

Addison directed her attention—and a brittle smile—to Ben. "We're all models, only some of us are more representative of the market we serve. Full-figured, curvy women who prefer not to be labeled as whales and shunted off to a forgotten corner of the lingerie section of department stores or specialty boutiques. It's hard for bigger gals to get breast support without sacrificing the sexy. Why not have both?"

Ben dipped his gaze to her chest and murmured, "Why not indeed?"

Okaaay. So he responded more to the verbal. She tried to refocus the conversation.

"The design part is my favorite. Picking fabrics, silhouettes, trimmings. But the business aspect is more fun than I expected. I like bargaining, trying to get my line into stores, bringing attention to something that makes a woman feel her best."

Harper chimed in. "That shouldn't be a problem with your pedigree. You've made other people's bras and knickers look good. You're a name to be trusted in the biz."

Addison certainly hoped so. Her eponymous line, *Beautiful by Addison*, aimed at full-figured women, would be unveiled in time for the holiday shopping season. When a man went into Macy's to buy his wife, girlfriend, or mistress a sexy gift, she prayed *Addison* would be the name on his lips. And if it was the name in his head when he uncovered his lady later, then so be it. Addison was fully aware of the fantasy she was selling with that balconette bra and barely there thong.

"So are you going to be modeling the underwear, Addy?"

Addison's eyes shot up at the questioner: the hockey player wearing a completely serious expression. Irritation pitched her internal organs into a storm, though the warm way he said her name gave other parts of her anatomy a flutter of caution. He shouldn't run his tongue over her name like he was tasting it—and her with it.

"Would you have a problem with that?"

Shit, she hadn't meant to sound so testy or imply she cared if he cared. She meant men in general. Men such as her husband, who objected to her modeling as soon as he shackled her.

With this ring, I thee wed.

With this ring, thy career is dead.

Callaghan held her gaze, far too intimately for someone who had supposedly just met her. "Some guys don't like seeing their woman showing that much skin to the public."

Oh, for fuck's sake. Trust a Neanderthal goon to have a brain as big as one of his nads. He truly was her husband's man.

Ignoring the brawny lump, she turned to the accountant. "What about you, Ben? Would it bother you if your woman showcased her 38 Double Ds"—*that's right, boys, they're real and they're spectacular*—"in sexy lace and silks to pimp her clothing line?"

Ben picked up his glass of wine and sipped, then gulped. She tried to imagine him between her legs, working her over with his tongue, while his frosty-tipped Faux-hawk bobbed up and down. Would it be stiff with hair product? Would it split apart to reveal a shiny pate if she grabbed it?

Would he look up and surprise her because he wasn't Ford Callaghan?

Stop it!

Ben set the glass down carefully. "My wife wouldn't need to work."

Ah, please fuck off forever, Ben.

Her eyes snapped to Callaghan and found a mischief she couldn't appreciate in his dark caramel-hued gaze.

"Is that how you feel, Mr. Callaghan?" He smirked at how she addressed him, and even that was sexy on him. "Should a wife be hidden away, relying on her husband's financial support, keeping her best lingerie for his eyes only?"

Just as her ex-husband had decreed. And to think she had listened to him as he insisted he'd "take care of her." Remembrance of those days spiked her Irish, not because Michael had a warped view of modern marriage, but because she had allowed him to dictate the terms. She'd turned down lucrative contracts so he wouldn't have to endure social media commentary about how his half-naked wife made her living.

She was to be *his* trophy, a prize for him alone.

"If my woman wanted to show the world how talented and beautiful she was, then she could be wearing a Snuggie for all I care. But if she'd rather do it wearing lingerie on a catwalk, I'd have no problem with that. Whatever makes her happy and fulfilled. If it contributes to our household bottom line, all the better."

Evolved *and* annoying. He had deliberately poked her to set her up. Likely, he had heard the rumors about her ex-husband not appreciating his wife's own efforts to contribute to the household bottom line.

She scowled again. Ford blasted her with a smile that

made her furious. She was not enjoying this, not at all. Caught off guard was not a good look on her.

Harper coughed significantly. "Addy, could you help me for a second in the kitchen?"

"Sure!"

Harper double-frowned at Addison's uncharacteristic enthusiasm.

Smiling like a clown at Ben and sparing not a crumb of attention for Callaghan, Addison followed her friend into the amazingly appointed kitchen where Harper had never cooked a thing in her life. The woman wasn't really the "keep the home fires burning" type. As one of professional sport's potentially most powerful business owners —if her father would loosen the reins and have a little faith—she would never have been satisfied playing meek housewife.

It wasn't completely inaccurate to say that Addison wanted to be Harper when she grew up.

Addison opened her mouth to apologize, but Harper got there first. "I'm so sorry about Ford. This has got to be awkward, him being on Michael's team and all."

Girl, you have no idea.

"It's fine." Her voice pitched a smidge too high. "Really, I'm okay. Like I said, Michael and I are ancient history."

Harper looked how Addison felt. Unconvinced.

"So what do you think of Ben? He'd make a good . . . lap dog?"

Addison laughed, then covered her mouth guiltily.

"He's quite nice despite the throwback statements about his wife not needing to work."

Harper waved that off. "Sometimes the nice ones are demons in the sack. No doubt he'd be working hard at the downtown station making sure the trains run on time.

Would treat you like a queen, but grateful, y'know? He'd never stray, not with a hot mama like you warming his bed."

"You're really selling it. Alas, I'd crush him with my thighs."

Laughing, Harper picked up a glass of wine on the counter and sipped it. She liked to leave spare glasses everywhere so she was never long without. Not judgin', just sayin'.

"Ford called you Addy. Sort of familiar."

"He's got some nerve."

Harper's eyes narrowed in suspicion, but instead of questioning Addison's overreaction, she mused, "Pity about his connection to Michael because I think he might be man enough for you."

That's what she was afraid of. She couldn't remember being so affected by such a masculine presence. For two years while married to Michael, she'd spent plenty of time at parties and events filled with strapping jocks and walking muscle factories. There was no good reason why this one should be different than any other.

Apart from the voice that teased an illicit orgasm from her.

But it wasn't just what the voice unlocked or the inhibition it had dissolved. Addison would never forget the reverence. How special and beautiful and *complete* he had made her feel. Ridiculous, because she knew she was all those things, and didn't need a man to validate her. But it had been wonderful to be the focus of this stranger's attention. His wonder.

To be seen so intimately without being seen at all.

But now he was here in the light, and his focus no longer felt so liberating. She hadn't liked how he'd watched her across the dinner table, those dark eyes filled with carnal knowledge, those sensuous lips goading her into a defense of her right to earn a goddamn living.

I know what makes you feel good, those eyes said. *I know you like it a little bit dirty. A whole lot dangerous.*

There was no safety in his presence. He had thoroughly seduced her without laying a finger on her body and now she was falling under his spell again. She needed to gather her wits and work up a plan that didn't involve going ten rounds of foreplay with Ford "Killer" Callaghan.

5

As soon as Harper came back without Addy, Ford made his move. He had to get her alone. Either he left the room and sought her out or he stayed and punched out the guy Harper had set Addy up with. So the accountant hadn't done anything except be in the wrong place at the wrong time; Ford was all for giving him a chance to stay out of the way of his fist.

He should have put two and two together when he heard her name, but she and Babineaux had divorced before Ford landed on the Cajun Rage sixteen months ago. Of course before that, everyone had known who she was—who wouldn't know about Addison Williams, the first woman who wasn't a negative size four to be featured on the cover of *Sports Illustrated's Swimwear Issue*? She was already a big deal, but that spread rocketed her into every heterosexual male's spank bank. During college, he'd had a picture of her inside his locker. She had helped him pass many a lonely night and last night she'd done it again.

With just her voice.

But there was more to it than that. Sure, she was a knockout with flawless olive skin, bright moss-green eyes, honey-brown waves that fell over her shoulders (he'd guessed wrong about her being a brunette), and more curves than the Daytona Speedway. All that was gravy to her wry humor and obvious passion about her career. He loved hearing how fired up she got about it—after spending years fending off women looking to use him as a meal ticket, Addy's independence and comfort in her own skin was more attractive to him than her perfect set of measurements.

Pity this was a disaster in the making. Ex or not, she was still one of Babineaux's Babes, as his harem of women were labeled by the sports media, even if her membership had expired. While playing for Houston a couple years ago, Ford had spotted her in the owner's box at rink-level. His breath had whooshed from his body at seeing his schoolboy fantasy in the flesh, then trapped in his lungs at seeing Babineaux with a hand on her leg, announcing to all that she belonged to him.

She'd looked uncomfortable. Lonely.

Or perhaps, that was wishful thinking and plenty revisionist because even then, Ford would rather have been the one possessing her.

So she was his boss's ex. Babe Prime. He didn't know what happened between them beyond the man's inability to satisfy his woman in the bedroom. What else he knew? He had to talk to her alone.

He hovered near the staircase for a few moments, expecting that was the best way to catch her, and it wasn't long before he was rewarded. She emerged from a room farther down the hallway, frowning when she saw him.

He moved to meet her. "Where are you staying?"

In Skates Trouble

"Here." She grimaced, probably not intending to be so forthcoming, and that made him smile. With a nervous motion, she smoothed her hands over her skirt, a voluminous crimson affair that hit above her knees.

It would look mighty fine up around her hips.

He gentled her back into the room she'd exited, a bathroom, and shut the door behind him.

"We need to talk, Addy."

Green almond-shaped eyes flashed fire. "No, we don't. I told you nothing would happen again. It wouldn't have anyway, and it especially won't now."

"Not sure I can be satisfied with that answer." He leaned in and inhaled her. Something sweet and floral. Very sexy. "Can you?"

"The others . . . we have to get back . . ." She loosed a growl of annoyance, tinged with something like helplessness. "You need to let me go."

Hell. He wasn't in the habit of forcing unwanted attentions on a woman. Crowding her like this was inappropriate, so he stepped back, creating a clear path to exit.

"I'm sorry. I just—Addy, I needed to touch you. See if you were real. Imagining your taste has left me with no appetite for anything else. I'm sure the dinner is great, but damned if I know."

Thoughts chased each other across her face before finally settling on determination. Shit, he'd blown it by coming on so strong.

Her hand strayed to the doorknob, a subtle shake in it, and she paused. With her other hand, she placed gentle fingertips on his chest, then flattened her palm against him. Like she was checking if *he* was real. Her heat through his shirt burned him with her brand.

"This is all wrong," she whispered, her eyes wild with

emotion. "Do you realize you're putting your career in jeopardy or," her brow crimped, "or is this some weird strategy to get one over on my ex?"

Anger flared. He grasped her hips and pulled her close until she was right against his "strategy."

"Does that feel like I care about my career?"

The words coming out of his mouth made no sense. In this moment, there was no Cup or Rajuns or Michael Babineaux. There was only her.

She was breathing heavily, the rise of her breasts straining against a top that covered her all too well, but fired his imagination and memories of her as the pin-up of his fantasies. He wanted those tits filling his mouth until he came from her taste.

Bright eyes beating with desire, she strained closer, as if she couldn't help the movements of her body.

"Fuck, Addy, what are you doing to me?"

"I—I can't think around you."

Neither could he, and he suspected clarity would not help this situation any. He grasped her ass and yanked her hard against him, then he made sure his mouth gave her something to think about. Her lips moved softly against his, then opened to accept him, her tongue's velvet slide whipping up spirals of need throughout his body. The taste of her blew his mind, a million times better than his brain could have imagined.

And he'd spent close to twenty-four hours in a fever of imagining.

She clutched at his button-down. He'd debated getting dressed up and now he was glad he had, because a woman like this would be used to a sharp-dressed man. She wouldn't stand for a scruffy skater on her arm.

Not sure why that thought had even entered his dumb brain, he aimed for dumbing down his brain even further in the pursuit of mindless pleasure. The kiss dragged him in, pushed him under, ruined him for all others.

They parted, both of them panting hard. Her full, soft breasts smashed against his chest. He liked that she was tall and they aligned in all the right places.

"What are we—? Oh, God." Those eyes shone like big headlights.

"Call me Ford, Bright Eyes. Say my name."

"No." She dug into his shoulders, an additional marking. Every touch was a barb under his skin that couldn't be detached. "No names. No cutsey monikers. It's bad enough what happened last night. There wasn't supposed to be a follow-up. It was supposed to end on a nice note and—"

"A nice note, Addy? You're calling the best orgasms we've ever had *nice*?"

She canted her head, wryness in the motion. "Speak for yourself, Callaghan."

His last name, but a victory nonetheless. He loved how she was trying her best to stand up to him, grasping at the straws of her slipping control. She wouldn't be a pushover, not like the women who hung out at bars close to the arena looking to get laid by a champion.

"Tell me that wasn't the hottest thing you've ever done, Addy." He backed her against the vanity. As befitting a fixture in a mansion belonging to Harper Chase, it looked plenty roomy for what he'd love to do. Marble, too, so all class. "Tell me touching yourself while I stroked one out in the dark didn't take you to places you've never traveled before."

She bit down on her lip, let the moment ride. Like she

was thinking back to her résumé of orgasms and weighing last night's against them.

Maybe that one? No, not as intense.

Maybe that time when he . . . ? No, not as explosive.

Maybe the . . . ? Oh, not even close.

Too fucking right. He couldn't help the smile that conquered his face.

"Quit looking so damn smug."

He curled a hand around her neck. "Ain't smug if I've got the tools to back it up, now, is it?" A roll of his hips against hers made it clear he had the tools.

She groaned at the connection, at the blatant display of his need. *This is how much I want you, baby.*

Pulling at his collar, she drew him close to her mouth. "I'm going to regret this—" And then she ended that sentence with a searching kiss filled with heat and not an ounce of regret.

Backed-into-a-corner Addy kissed pretty damn fine, but all-in Addy was another thing entirely. A force of nature, a typhoon in this tiny space.

Another hook into his soul.

Fuck. Me.

"Please. Oh, God, please, I need . . ." He thought she meant for him to touch her, but she grasped at the zipper to his jeans and pulled it down. She was that desperate to get her hands on his dick and hell if that didn't make him as hard as the marble he wanted to fuck her on.

Her hand shook as she yanked his jeans south, his boxer briefs with them. He didn't help her, even though every urge in him wanted to hurry this along. The winning urge, however, wanted her to make the decisions. No one would be confused later about the choice made here.

His would be the name on her lips when she came. His touch alone would bring her the satisfaction she craved.

She gripped the erection she'd sprung free and inhaled a wobbly breath.

"This is what I missed last night."

Christ, she was touching him at last. "It missed you. Needed you. Imagined your hand stroking hard while I tongued between your legs. Reality is a million times better."

Her eyes flipped up from watching her hand do exactly what he'd imagined. Blood surged through his body at what he saw in her gaze. The power she harnessed, now that she'd accepted his desire for her, was an unstoppable force.

With her eyes locked on his, she continued to work him, using the pre-come beading from his crown to ease the glide of her soft hands.

Yeah, reality was beating fantasy into submission.

"Addy," he grunted, then yanked at the folds of her skirt, pushing it up over her hips while at the same time seating her on the vanity. The pretty cream fabric shielding her core wasn't wispy or transparent, yet he knew it wouldn't hold up under his assault. He could rip it but it felt like some sort of sacrilege.

She was watching him carefully, and he hazarded a guess why. "Your design?"

"Yes. Seamless hipster with lace trim." She urged him forward, her hand still gripping him, his cock on her leash, and painted a line of his pre-cum along the fabric, right where the crease of her pussy would be if she were bare. There was something unbelievably sensual about the fact this was happening against a beautiful thing she had created. Those sexy panties she'd designed, the ones covering her curves, now wore his mark.

It felt like they were making something together.

"Jesus." The sensation of the soft, silky material against his cockhead was exquisite. Or maybe it was the fact she was dragging it back and forth, using him to get herself stoked.

He was going to blow if he didn't get inside her soon. "Now."

Maneuvering her body to get better access, he dragged the panties down and it was just as she'd described, a little landing strip, but better, so much better, because she was here consuming his every sense.

"Tell me you have a condom."

"I have a condom." He un-pocketed his wallet and extracted the foil. While he smoothed it on, she watched approvingly.

"Take off your shirt," she whispered, and because he would have done a jig if she asked him to, he peeled it off.

Her hands flew to his pecs, coasted across his shoulders. "So big," she murmured. She trailed soft fingertips down his arms until she reached his hands. Against his left, she measured her own palm. It barely made up half the surface area of his hand.

"I hoped they'd be big. I hoped you'd be big every-where." Her sleepy-lidded gaze dropped to his jutting cock, huge and ready for her. It felt bigger than it ever had, engorged by the sight before him and the need pumping through his body like rocket fuel.

With the big hands she liked, he pulled her to the edge of the vanity, nudging against her slick entrance before he drove in deep and true. Just the sheer greedy-hot grip of her dragged a roar from him.

"Oh God, oh God, oh God," she panted.

He withdrew and plunged again, balls deep, mesmerized as her eyes exploded into mini-suns of passion. Alternating

In Skates Trouble 45

between watching her and watching his cock disappear inside her was incomparable. Need had a catch on him, keeping him in a state of "fuck her to oblivion or die in the process." Either result would be fine as long as he could feel her walls milk him to an explosive end.

This was where he wanted to be. This was what he'd been holding out for, the connection he'd longed for. *This.* And still, it didn't feel deep enough. He cupped one perfect ass cheek, strayed his hand to the back of her thigh, and lifted to increase the angle of penetration. Only an extra inch, but it sent her eyes rolling to the back of her head.

"Jesus, that's . . ." Her admiration was cut off by another punishing thrust. So deep. So tight. The slick sound of juicy suction filled his ears, as did the heightening octaves of her groans.

Watching that plunge home again and again, each withdrawal showing his dick coated with her desire for him, made him wilder than he'd ever been for a woman. Was it the taboo they were breaking? Who they were to each other? Where they had chosen to fuck hard, wet, and deep?

As if there'd been a choice.

Because there wasn't for him. That voice and dry wit of hers had drawn him in and nothing could have stopped him from joining his body to hers in reality. Not her identity. Not a dinner table spat about gender politics that turned him on more than off. Not this inescapable breach of guest etiquette.

He wanted her, he was having her, and he would have her again.

"Please. Ford. Too much," she moaned. "Too much."

Placing the heel of his hand over her clit, he pressed with an upward stroke that sent her crashing over with a scream that must have shattered the chandelier in Harper's salon. The resulting clamp around his cock almost killed him—he held on a moment to delay because it kept him buried in heaven, and then he let go. Pounding the orgasm out of her to prolong her high, and taking his own as a reward for bringing them both so much pleasure.

6

ADDISON WALKED into the kitchen at chez Chase and almost buckled under the all-seeing gaze of Harper. Her friend stood at the kitchen island, dressed in tailored city shorts, a sleeveless teal silk blouse, and Cole Haan peep-toe wedges. No such thing as schlubbing on the weekend for Harper—she was ultra conscious of the image she had to maintain as an almost-CEO of an almost-world-class sports brand. Addison, on the other hand, preferred yoga pants and T-shirts on her days off. People never recognized her with her clothes on, anyway.

"Morning," she murmured and headed to the Keurig. Hmm, lots of lovely flavors . . .

"How does it feel?" her friend asked.

"How does what feel?"

"Ford Callaghan's massive—"

"Harper . . ."

"Stick," she finished with malevolent glee.

"I should never have said a word to you." Addison grabbed the almond mocha K-cup and popped it into the cradle of the machine.

"You had no choice. When a woman returns to the dinner table with stubble rash and a look of immense satisfaction, quickly followed by a man who is a lot smugger than a guy in my house has a right to be, she can hardly expect to get away without a little interrogation." She cupped her mouth with her hands. "So, you know when I said *stick*, I meant *cock*, right? That's hockey humor."

Addison skewered her with a look over her shoulder. "Your grandparents would turn in their graves if they could hear your language, Harper Chase."

"Are you kidding? Nana taught me all the best swear words before the age of five. She wanted me armed for the playground. And stop trying to change the subject."

"It was a one-off. Won't be happening again."

Of all Addison's friends, Harper understood best the danger she courted by getting involved with a player on her ex-husband's team. Michael might not have the legal grounds to fire Ford, but he could make things very difficult for his star right winger.

Harper studied her. "It is a rather awkward set of circumstances, I have to say."

"Even without the obvious problem of Michael being his boss, I'm not looking for a relationship right now. I want to focus on the new line, on getting settled in Chicago. Dating is not on my agenda—"

Harper scoffed.

"*Dating*," Addison insisted, "is not on my agenda. Not with balding accountants, and especially not with a big brute of a hockey player who's old enough to be my . . . younger brother."

"He's what? Twenty-six? Six years is nothing. You're only as old as the man you're feeling up. Besides . . ." She hesitated.

"Besides what?"

"You like him. I could tell at the dinner table before you sullied my first-floor guest bathroom with your hot 'n' heavy fuckfest. When's the last time you actually *liked* a guy?"

Addison blushed, though she wasn't sure if it was Harper's salty language or the accusation of liking Ford. She did like him.

"I don't know a thing about him." Except for what was on his Wikipedia page, which she'd read three times last night, along with a shit ton of media coverage he'd garnered in the last few years. He'd built an amazing career since being drafted for Philly eight years ago, though he was with the New Orleans Rage for only one amazing season when everything had come together and they'd gone all the way. Their paths had never crossed. She liked to think she would have remembered those soft, chocolate-drop eyes, the messy, rakeable hair, and his goofy-cocky grin. After her divorce, she'd put herself on a media embargo regarding all things related to Michael. No hockey, no sports pages, nothing.

"What do you want to know?" Harper considered her shrewdly, a glint of mischief sparking her eyes.

"Nothing. I don't want to . . ." She stopped, remembering something from the Wikipedia page. Something that gnawed at her. "He had a brother who died."

"Paul Callaghan. Best NCAA center I've ever seen, number-one pick in the draft that year. Toronto got him but he never even saw a game. Traffic accident the night before he was due to start."

How awful. But there was more. Ford and another brother had been in the car. The other brother—Jackson?—was injured as well. A promising talent, the news articles reported at the time, but there was no mention of him making it to pro level.

"Ford was driving," Addison said, repeating what she'd learned online. He would have been young, sixteen years old. Old enough to drive but not old enough to weather what came after. That must have been gut-wrenching for him.

"I've no doubt it was," Harper replied.

So Addison had spoken that aloud. But it needed to be said, didn't it?

"And now he has the Cup," Harper added when Addison remained silent.

Addison stared at her friend. "Hardly a consolation."

"You'd be surprised," Harper said, her voice taking on a firm quality while her thoughts seemed to send her somewhere beyond the room. "Winning wipes out a lot of pain."

"Go for the face, boys."

Jackson's voice was barely audible over the shouts of Ford's three nephews as they tackled him to the ground. He'd considered bringing the Cup for a visit but now he was glad he hadn't. Not that the trophy couldn't handle it—that hunk of metal got a serious pounding on the post-Finals tour every year—but these kids might have bonked their heads or cut their lips. Ford couldn't stand the notion of them getting hurt.

He lay still in the grass on his brother's front lawn in Bridgeport on Chicago's South Side, enjoying the moment of normalcy before he had to sit up and face the obvious tension when you don't visit your family much—or ever.

Seven-year-old Coby sat on his chest while Petie, eight

In Skates Trouble

going on eighty, had Ford pinned by the arm. Mikey, just turned six and the smartest one, was already unzipping Ford's duffel looking for the goods. He whipped out a Rajuns jersey.

"Aw, this is so cool, Uncle Ford!" His bright eyes sparked anew with each additional team member signature he came across on his visual journey from neck to hem.

"Michael James Callaghan," Marcy yelled, "stop rifling through your uncle's crap."

"What's rifling?" Coby asked.

Ford grinned at his sister-in-law. "It's all right." He'd seen the kids at away games in Chicago over the last couple years, but had missed watching them grow up, and there was something achingly everyday about how they made themselves right at home with his stuff. Guilt flooded his chest. That was on him.

All three signed jerseys had been pulled out along with his underwear, clothes, shaving kit, and . . . condoms. Marcy yanked the boys away with one hand and repacked his duffel with the other in that efficient way moms had. On depositing the condoms back in the bag, she smirked and he smirked right back, the good-natured exchange giving him a needed moment to get his shit together and face his brother.

They'd never been huggers, and they sure as hell wouldn't be starting now. Jax held out his hand and Ford clasped it firmly, though his brother gripped harder, probably to prove something. At just twenty-eight, he was two years older than Ford but looked ten. Whiskey and kids aged a man something fierce.

"Thanks for letting me stay," Ford said awkwardly.

Jax sniffed, and stared him down. "Where the hell else you gonna go when you come home? Some fancy hotel?"

Not going there.

Ford turned back to find Mikey and Coby carrying his duffel, looking like they might collapse under the weight of it. He moved in. "I've got that, fellas."

Marcy held up her hand. "I can't get them to do a lick of work. Let them do this."

Two hours later, Ford pushed his empty plate a few inches forward, sat back in his chair, and rubbed his belly, the universal sign of contentment after a good meal. That lasagna was out of this world.

"Marcy, if you're ever ready to leave all this, I'll make room for you in NOLA."

His sister-in-law chuckled, eying her husband slyly.

"Tempting. What do you think, Jax? Should I run off with your rich and famous brother?"

Jax circled his finger along the rim of the glass of pop. He hadn't touched a beer or anything stronger in three years. "He wouldn't know what to do with you. I never see him on TMZ with any models—something you want to tell us, Fordie?"

Ford laughed, enjoying this playful side of his brother. Felt like old times.

"Just not interested in some airhead piece of ass." Oops, not very respectful toward women. He met Marcy's eyes. "Sorry, Marce."

"Don't apologize to me. Apologize to airhead pieces of ass everywhere who are missing out on all this." She flourished a hand in his direction, drawing his chuckle. "But seriously, Ford. No one caught your eye?"

Oh, someone had. Someone who could be trouble for

his career . . . but damn she was trouble wrapped in a sweet package. Those gorgeous curves filling his hands as he filled her body, and the way she'd responded when he sank into her—soft and sexy, surrender and a burgeoning awareness of her unique power. He didn't think he'd forget that as long as he lived.

He really should stay away from her but he was having a hard time coming up with a God-honest reason.

"There is someone." Marcy dropped to the seat beside him and rested her chin on her hands, eyelids fluttering madly. "A man only smiles like that when he's thinking of a woman."

Jax dipped his head with a not-so-furtive glance below the table. "What's going on down south confirms it."

"For fuck's sake," Ford bit out, but Marcy just laughed her head off. Nothing could shock this woman, not after everything Jax had put her through. They'd had some tough years while his brother looked for the solution to his problems in a bottle of Jack.

Recognizing that Ford wasn't going to fess up about his mystery woman, Marcy sighed dramatically, stood, and walked to the bottom of the stairs. "Five minutes," she shouted up, "and then you'd better be brushing your teeth or Uncle Ford's gonna leave right now."

Ford heard the scramble-pound of three sets of feet and the oomph of little brothers being tortured by bigger ones. It turned him inside out with memories of Paulie and Jax.

Marcy rolled her eyes indulgently. "I'd better make sure they get a move on." She left the room, probably deliberately to give them privacy.

Ford slid a glance toward his brother, disappointed to find any trace of levity gone and in its place something he couldn't quite label. No, that wasn't right. Ford knew what it was. It was the same message that crossed his brother's face anytime he looked at Ford.

You might have it all now, Fordie, but you fucked up big time on your way.

"Been a while," Jax said.

Ford nodded. "Tickets were always waiting for you at the box office whenever I played in Chicago. While it's great to see the kids and Marcy, I would have been thrilled if you came to see me."

Jax stood and went to the fridge, holding the door open as if the mysteries of the universe could be unraveled with the explosion of light.

"Haven't watched a game in ten years, live or on TV," he said quietly. "Until six weeks ago."

Ford's breath caught. He knew how his brother felt about hockey. That pin in his leg reminded him every day how much he'd lost that night. Not just Paulie, the guy who could have been as good as Gretzky, but his own hopes and dreams for an amazing career.

"How'd I do?"

Jax grabbed a big bottle of Coke from the fridge, poured a half glass, then sat at the table again. Drawing it out, he was, and Ford waited, his heart in a stall.

"You had three shots to score in game three and two in five and you held back. You were always too tentative in the crunch."

Okay. Ford accepted that. As kids, he'd paid more attention to Paulie because he was the oldest, and from mini-squirt all the way to junior AAA, he was the god who knew everything. But Paulie was dead and Jax had watched a hockey game for the first time in ten years.

Fucking hell.

"It's faster than you think on pro ice."

Jax's eyes snapped up. "You think I don't know that?"

"I didn't mean—"

His brother waved it off, but Ford knew what he was doing. Controlling the conversation as he had done for the last ten years. Everything was on his terms because he was the aggrieved party.

"What, Fordie?" The query emerged dripping with sarcasm. "You too much of a big shot to take your brother's advice?"

"You're not giving advice. You're picking a fight. But you can't even do that right." Ford blew out a breath.

Killing the number-one draft pick the night before he was due to start his pro career was not how Ford wanted to be remembered. When that pick was your oldest brother and you destroyed the future of your other brother in the process, that was an even harder pill to swallow.

The worst, though? Not only would Jax never forgive him, Ford would never forgive himself. That night, he'd lost both his brothers, not just one.

Ford looked around the homey kitchen, filled with cookbooks and pots, plants and bric-a-brac. Drawings and postcards clung tentatively to the fridge door with magnets, one of them with the Rajuns logo, a crawfish holding a hockey stick in its right claw and a beignet in the other. Dumbest logo ever. This place wasn't unlike the house they'd grown up in four blocks over, though their parents were long gone. A fitting home for a man on a city-of-Chicago salary. The money Ford sent to Marcy was spent on the kids.

He'd buy his brother a mansion if he would accept it. He'd do anything to relieve his pain. Raw bitterness tinged the air between them. Ford would rather they fought it out, but he didn't want to upset the kids or Marcy.

"How's work?" Ford asked, though that was another minefield. Literally.

"Perfect. I finish filling in holes on one street then go back to the beginning and start over. Job security's a cinch in the pothole capital of the United States."

"You should be coaching over at Rebels youth hockey camp. They'd have you in a heartbeat."

Jax lifted his tee, showing how time had changed his formerly flatter-than-a-pancake abs. Once, you wouldn't have found an ounce of fat on that big frame.

"Cut out the soda and don't take an extra serving of Marcy's lasagna and you'd be back in shape before you knew it."

"Right. That's all it takes. Didn't ask for your advice."

"You've no problem giving it to me when you're watching my form." Although Ford would prefer the rough criticism if it meant his brother talked to him again. He'd take that call after every game.

"Well, don't worry, that's the last time I watch. You've got it now." *It*, being the Cup. *It*, being the life they'd all dreamed about every morning when they got up at four thirty to hit hockey practice before school.

"Jax—"

His brother held up his hand. "You stay out of my business and I'll stay out of yours."

He got up and blew the room, leaving Ford and his heart halfway to breaking.

7

DRINKING ALONE WAS PERFECTLY OKAY.

That ever-so-slightly judgy statement rang in Addison's ears as she tipped a bottle of red into her empty glass for the third time in the last hour. It wasn't her fault she was riding this fruity little number from the New World solo. Harper had abandoned her to attend some glitzy charity gala as Kenneth Bailey's date. That guy definitely had his eye on her as the future Mrs. Bailey, though Harper insisted they were just friends.

Since the divorce, Addison hadn't read a single word, seen a single picture, watched a single video of hockey even though she'd always loved the game. She and her brother Jamie were die-hard Spartans fans. Growing up in Brooklyn surrounded by the fan base of the rival Boulders, it was a risk they took. (And given the state of the Boulders these days, it was a risk that paid off.) So it was hard to give it up. But the thought of being faced with photos of Michael with a younger, slimmer model-of-the-week at every game had made the decision for her. Better for her sanity to totally exorcise him from her life, and hockey with him.

But after two years, she might be ready.

It wouldn't have anything to do with Ford Callaghan.

Clicking through the online reports of the Finals, she was struck by how often the right winger appeared in photos. Perhaps she was just acutely conscious of his outsize presence now she had seen him naked. Felt him naked. Desperate to minimize the heat blazing across her body at the memory of his perfect, chiseled body, she took another sip of her wine. No dice. X-rated images played back relentlessly. His fingers kneading her ass, his whispered dirty talk in her ear, his hard length rooting deep inside her.

Moving on.

He had scored four goals during the series and had the record for assists in all seven games, despite that being more typical of a center. A giver, in every way. *Zing!* She watched a few videos, marveling at the easy grace of a man so large. Skating often gave that illusion, but she'd noticed it in him the night on the balcony. Fluid, not lumbering. A man at ease with his big body.

Lost in visions of Ford and the magic he could create with those wonderful hands, it took her a moment to realize the doorbell was ringing. She remained still. What the hell? There was no one in the house but her, and whoever was out there either wanted to see Harper or was cold-calling, neither of which Addison could help them with.

Ten seconds later, it rang again, and Addison imagined she heard urgency in it. A short blast—and there it was again. Longer this time, a burst of "I'm not moving until you acknowledge me."

She walked to the foyer, slowly, not owing anything to the impatient caller, and silently hoping the time it took her to get there would be time used by the person on the other side of the door to just go away. Harper had a one-way video intercom near the door and Addison pressed the button to activate it.

Ford Callaghan stood on the doorstep, looking directly at the camera. Shit.

"Harper, I need to see Addy. Could you open up?"

Even through the barrier of technology, she could hear the hitch of desperation in his voice. He was upset.

She shouldn't know that. She shouldn't understand that nuanced change in the timbre of his voice, but she did. And that frightened her more than anything.

She also knew that if she opened this door, it could end only one way.

Just one more time. Once more to feel the pleasure only this man could give.

She pulled back the bolt, keeping her eye on the video to see if his expression changed. Looking for—ah, shit. Relief.

He stood on the doorstep, wearing jeans and a plain gray tee that was elevated to a work of art because of how lovingly it hugged his pectorals and broad shoulders.

"Callaghan, what are you—?"

She had no chance to finish because he took the words right out of her mouth. His lips crushed, his tongue twined with hers. There was no gentleness to it.

Somehow, she found herself three feet back in the foyer —he must have lifted all one hundred ninety-three pounds of her—with his hands on her ass. The door was kicked close. Damn, Harper would kill her if she found a boot print on that oak.

He was everywhere at once, but it wasn't enough. She needed to reciprocate, so she grabbed his hair, his shoulders, and his ass to just plain indulge. That's what she wanted to do—indulge in this delicious treat of Ford Callaghan. So, so bad for her but she'd spent her life defying convention for how a woman should look and behave. If ever there was a moment she should take pleasure as her right, it was now.

"Addy, baby . . ." He halted his kisses. "I needed to see you. Tonight . . . damn, tonight, I just needed to see you."

In those frayed words, she heard hurt. Something had happened to bring him here tonight. He'd chosen her to medicate his pain.

Before she could ask more—*why me? why now?*—he yanked her leggings down and grabbed her rear hard enough to leave a mark. "Love this ass. Love how it feels."

This ass. She should feel objectified. God knew she was fluent in the language of reduction to her measurements, her body parts, her so-called representation of BBW everywhere. But she was more. She knew that. She suspected Ford also knew it, but this rough, elemental version had primal desires that needed to be slaked.

This man wanted *this* woman. Needed her. In this moment, she was a great ass, stellar tits, and a riot of curves that pleased him.

As for how he pleased her? The man was six feet four inches of upright perfection. She pushed him back toward the door he'd slammed closed, stalking him with his T-shirt fisted in her greedy grasp. Over his head, she pulled and it got stuck for a couple seconds and he might have grunted at her enthusiasm—*sorry, sorry, it's okay*—and then, it was definitely okay. It was more than okay.

She managed a sound. More akin to a gurgle, really, and she wasn't particularly proud of it. But, you see, his chest had entered the scene from stage left and was stealing every line of her script. A sculpted model of beauty that gushed wetness between her legs.

He didn't give her time to enjoy it because he was

returning the favor, grabbing at her flimsy tank and tearing it apart. She would have just taken it off, if he'd asked or tugged, but his passion turned her on so much. She stood before him in tatters and her bra—not the prettiest one she owned but with breasts like hers, underwear couldn't compete.

He fell to his knees.

Oh, that was good.

With hands in a possessive grasp of her ass, he positioned his mouth over her damp satin-covered mound and sucked through the fabric right at the cleft.

That was more than good.

Her groan emerged full-throated, like an animal's.

Moving the fabric aside with his thumb, he licked, then seemed to realize that such limited access wasn't enough. Those panties didn't last another second.

Neither did her legs. Lingerie model down.

Luckily, there was a plush rug keeping her ass from meeting cold tile, and now it was just a frenzy of how to get completely naked in four seconds flat. *There, that, now, now.* Off came her leggings, down came his zipper, on went a condom, and then—yes, yes, *fuck, yes.* One long thrust and he was inside her, the stretch of her muscles perfect, the way they fit together so, so right.

He set up a steady rhythm of push and pull, invasion and retreat, and how the hell had she gone from Internet surfing to fucking a hockey player on Harper's Persian rug in the span of a few ragged breaths? Something had been set in motion that night on the balcony, and she wasn't sure how to go back to before—or if she even wanted to.

She was hooked.

His mouth crashed down over the plush mounds above her bra cup, before he nudged the silky barrier aside and drew her nipple into his mouth. This new source of pleasure near killed her. His suckle on her breast, his plunder between her legs, and then one hand clasped to her ample ass and squeezed hard. His other hand moved to her throat, holding her with a sure, but gentle grip, his thumb moving up to force her lips apart to complete the pillage. She was entirely immobilized, every part of her in his masculine grip. His control was absolute, his need intense.

She loved it. She loved giving him this.

The thrusts became less smooth, more jerky, and she recognized he might not be in as much control as she'd thought. But then neither was she.

He unlatched his mouth from her breast and affixed it to a place much more dangerous—the lips that were about two seconds away from screaming his name. Making this personal. It wasn't supposed to be this personal.

He's inside you. That's pretty damn personal, Addy.

Through soul-searing kisses and bone-melting stares, he pumped harder and faster, so hard and fast she worried he might burrow through to the wine cellar beneath their joined, sweaty bodies. A babble of mostly incoherent words gutted from him. She heard her name and "sogoodsogood" and then what was formerly the ass-owning hand became the clit-stroking hand. It glanced softly against her then pressed hard above the spot where they had become one and she left this world for another dimension.

There was no doubt whose name she shouted when she came. Now that she knew it and what its owner was capable of, she suspected it would always be his name on her lips.

She expected him to explode now that he'd taken care of her, but he seemed content to slow it down, almost as if he could relax now her pleasure was achieved.

That selflessness only hiked her desire further.

He rolled onto his back, pulling her with him, ensuring their bodies were still melded, and reached for her breasts with both hands. Hands big enough to cover her ample rack.

Had she mentioned she liked a guy with big hands?

This position was heaven, the penetration deeper, the view out of this world.

"That's it, Bright Eyes. Ride me to the end."

So she did, squeezing and slipping and sliding until she hit that pinnacle again, not knowing how, not caring why, and only then did he finally let go, emptying inside her, the force and heat palpable even with the condom.

She collapsed over his chest, her breasts happily smushed, her ear at the base of his throat listening to the pulse kicking hard against her cheek. Moments of precious quiet passed, the only noise their thunderous hearts and a sense of wonder at what was happening here.

Testing the waters, she shifted slightly, knowing she'd eventually have to unhinge from him. He held on tight.

Test passed.

"Stay. Just a little while longer," he whispered.

A plus, Callaghan.

BURIED IN ADDY.

Ford wanted to write a sappy song with that title. He could think of no place he'd rather be, and after the night he'd had, this felt like a much-needed sanctuary. He didn't want to think of his brother or the argument that brought him to Addy's door. Maybe because he didn't want to think he might have used her to shift that hurt from his heart to his dick.

But the reality of this journey to the best orgasm of his life, not to mention sex on the floor in a house belonging to neither of them, intruded. He assumed there was no one else at home, a state of affairs that would likely not last.

"Sweetheart, I should take care of business."

She lifted her head, honey-coppery strands curtaining her eyes. "You already did, Callaghan. Twice."

Hell, that made a man feel good.

She sat up and eased off him while he held the condom in place. This was going to be tricky . . .

Or not. She unrolled the rubber carefully and stood.

"Back in a sec."

He watched/ogled while she walked to the first-floor bathroom—scene of the crime last night and hey, look at them making more criminally sexy memories—and went inside. All while gloriously naked.

He liked that. The nakedness, natch, but the fact she took care of the rubber. Took care of him. It had been a while since someone had done that. Gave him hope that messy consequences were something she'd take in her stride.

And they had some exceedingly messy consequences right here.

She returned, grabbed the shirt he'd ripped from her body and held it up with a cute smirk of *that just happened*. She put it on backwards and it barely covered what he had just feasted on, then added the leggings. Standing, he pulled up the jeans he'd shoved to only mid-thigh because he wasn't fuckin' around.

Wordlessly, she led him by the hand to a room just off the main hallway, a cozy living space he hadn't seen on his party-crash last night. A laptop was open along with a bottle of wine, a glass of red half-gone.

"Now, tell me about your day," she said, gesturing at the sofa.

He laughed at her no-nonsense take on it. "All that matters is how it ended."

She sat, curling her legs under her body, compassion shining off her. He wanted to lay his head on those gorgeous breasts and fall asleep.

"Callaghan."

"You can call me Ford."

"Have a seat, Callaghan."

He did, though her reluctance to use his first name rankled. When his tongue had delved inside her body, she'd shouted it out. When she shuddered and shook around his cock, she'd screamed it loud. He'd get it again from her before the night was through.

"Glass of wine?"

"I don't drink. I come from a long line of alcoholics so I prefer not to risk it."

She nodded. "Something upset you tonight."

"It's nothin'. Just family stuff."

Those gorgeous eyes of hers carved right through him, so he looked away, not enjoying the scrutiny. It was one thing to be locked in those crosshairs while inside her, but outside of sex, the exposure was less of a comfort. His gaze fell on her open laptop and the big image of Ford Callaghan hugging . . . team owner Michael Babineaux.

Babineaux wasn't exactly a friend—their relationship was more complicated than that. While there was nothing in his contract that said he couldn't screw the boss's ex-wife, Ford knew that the legal niceties would not prevent Babineaux from making his life a living hell. Trading him would be an option but the boss wouldn't go that easy on him. More likely, he would play out the rest of his two-year contract warming the pine.

But only if he found out. Which he wouldn't.

"Catching up on your reading?"

She flicked a glance to the laptop. "I haven't been following hockey much in the last couple of years. Not since the divorce."

"And now you are."

Her look said it all. *This is madness.*

"You think I shouldn't have come."

She peeked up at him through long, golden-brown lashes. "No, you shouldn't have. But you did and then you did. Come, that is. You needed to be here and now . . ." She placed a hand on his chest. "What happened before can't *unhappen*, but neither can it happen again. What I can do is listen. Whatever's got you all twisted up, I can hear you."

His heart rumbled like a jet engine in his chest, the effect of her touch, her nearness, both incitement and salve. Christ, he wanted to tell her everything.

"Addy, I'm—"

The sound of the door opening forced them apart. They both turned to the inevitable appearance of the lady of the house. There was no good way to explain why he was sitting in Harper Chase's living room with a beautifully flushed Addison Williams, draped in a ripped-to-shreds tank.

"Oh, hello, Ford," Harper said over-brightly. "In the neighborhood, were you?"

Addison pointed at Harper. "Can it, Chase. He's leaving." She took his hand and led him past Harper, who held his gaze with an arched raise of her eyebrow. He didn't know her well, but he knew a smart-ass when he saw one.

At the door, Addison stopped, still holding his hand. "I meant what I said."

"No more sex on hallway rugs."

"*What?*" An out-of-hearing-range Harper was apparently not the same as an out-of-sight Harper.

"Have a drink, Harper," Addison called out, cool as the other side of the pillow before turning back to Ford. "That, and I'm here if you need to talk."

He didn't want to talk. He wanted her body lying next to him while he kissed every inch of it. He wanted to lose himself inside her until they both forgot who they were because if they could do that, all their problems would be solved. Maybe world hunger and peace in the Middle East while they were at it.

She wanted to talk.

Ladies and gentlemen: the difference between men and women in a nutshell.

"Give me your number." At her frown, he added, "The exchange of phone numbers is the best way to prevent further exchange of bodily fluids."

She laughed, and he loved that sound. Loved that he'd produced it.

"I would think exchanging phone numbers would lead to the other type of exchange."

"Not the way we've been doing it. But then this isn't exactly conventional." He grinned, feeling strangely better that they were able to make jokes of it. Then it hit him.

He wouldn't be able to touch her again.

She had decided that the complication of her ex being his boss was a bridge too far. The potential of *them*—of Ford and Addy—was not enough to overcome that obstacle.

It seemed to dawn on her at the same time, or at least, he chose to credit that wrinkle of her brow to the state of suckage they had both found themselves in.

"Your number, Addy?" There was a little grit in his tone

because hell and damn, he was not leaving without that number.

She hesitated for a soul-numbing moment, but then rattled it off. He nodded, memorizing each digit, the way her mouth shaped it, and the sexy clamp of her lovely white teeth on her bottom lip when she was done.

"Not going to put it in your phone?"

"I won't forget it." And if he did—if he chose to—it would be because self-preservation beat his cock to the mat.

Before his libido got the better of him again, he left without another word.

Addison put on her game face and headed into the living room, where Harper was seated on the sofa with brows drawn and mouth pinched. She patted the seat cushion beside her.

"Let's chat, honey."

Blowing out a breath, Addison sat down beside her and launched into her defense. "You're right, I have no idea what I'm doing here."

"He's got it bad."

"He has?"

Harper gestured at the open laptop, still showing that photo of Ford hugging her ex as they celebrated the Finals win.

"This is his career and yet he's willing to risk it for a fling. Unless, he wants . . ."

"What?"

Harper cocked her head. "More."

Time to shut that nonsense down. "He does not want more. Tonight, he was upset and there's no risk of Michael

In Skates Trouble   69

finding out. It's not as if we've been seen in public." They wouldn't be either.

"You gave him your number."

There was that. "I think he needs someone to talk to."

Harper could make a career out of those eyebrow scoots.

"He does. And it's not as if Michael will check his players' phones." *Hell*. "Would he?"

"I make my players take regular drug tests. Monitoring their phones isn't such a stretch." She grinned to let Addison know she was kidding. "Seriously, though. I'm thrilled you're getting some long-needed action, Addy, but could you not have chosen someone less unsuitable?"

"Well, if I'd known the first time . . ." Another eyebrow of judgment. Addison had filled Harper in on the down 'n' dirty details of her first *meeting* with Ford, and was now wishing she'd been a bit more circumspect. "It's done. I won't ever see him again. And now that I've gotten back on the horse—"

"A well-hung horse."

"Stop. It. I'll be able to jump right into dating once I'm settled in Chicago." Dating someone suitable: older, more stable, and most definitely not an employee of her husband.

A secretive smile lifted one corner of Harper's mouth. "I'll draw up a list immediately."

8

EDWIN "DON'T-CALL-ME-EDDIE" Motz whipped out the rag he carried everywhere and rubbed at some imaginary smudge on the Cup. Guy treated it like a mom cleaning off schmutz from her kid's cheek, except whereas Ford's mom would have used God's natural cleaner—the old tissue-saliva combo—Edwin would never dream of sullying the Cup with his bodily fluids.

He was about the only one who held it in such high regard.

The stories Ford had heard curled his toes. People feeding their family, friends, and dogs right out of the Cup. Players baptizing their kids in it. Fuckwits taking a piss in it. It had been mistreated for years, yet like the class act it was, it came up shining new every year. And that was mostly down to the Keeper of the Cup, Edwin Motz.

"Looks good, Edwin."

The guy peered at him through his oversized glasses. Ford felt certain that if Edwin had a choice on whether to push Ford or the Cup out of the way of a runaway truck, Ford's funeral would get a semi-decent turnout.

"She's ready to be seen," Edwin said with tremendous gravity.

Waiting outside was a bevy of kids, parents, club staff, and media who had gathered at the Chicago Pirates rink, the Tier I junior hockey club where Ford had honed his blades before going to Vermont and playing NCAA. Most of the guys took the Cup back to where it all started for them and Ford was no exception. The Pirates club was where each of the Callaghans had become men.

The door opened and Sean O'Hurley, his old coach, put his head around the door. "Got some visitors for ya, Fordie." His name was barely out of Sean's mouth, and his nephew Mikey bounded in, closely followed by Coby and Petie.

The sight of the Cup rendered them speechless. As it should.

"So that's what it takes to shut them up," Marcy said, walking in behind them with Jax.

Ford spared a smile for Marcy and a nod for his brother. He'd left early this morning so they hadn't talked since last night. Since before he'd gone to see Addy.

What had he been thinking? Just attacking her like a lion taking down a gazelle the minute he crossed the threshold. And not just any threshold either. Harper Chase's home. One word in one ear and Ford would be fucked, and not in a nice way.

But he didn't think Harper would do that. She was Addy's friend, and she had never struck Ford as malicious.

Perhaps he'd text Addy later, check in and make sure she wasn't suffering from a severe case of rug burn on that gorgeous rear of hers. Christ, that ass was a work of art and hell if it didn't fit his palms just right.

He looked down, newly conscious that Mikey was speaking while Ford's thoughts had shot over the plexi.

"What's that, kid?"

"Can we touch it?"

"You bet you can. Try lifting it if you want."

Edwin shot Ford a look, so he quickly put the Keeper at ease. "Just kidding, Eddie, they'd never—"

Shit. Ford just about managed to get to the Cup before it toppled over and crushed one or more of his nephews.

"Jesus," Jax said, but there was humor in it. He grabbed Mikey by the collar. "That weighs as much as you. At least forty pounds."

"Thirty-four-point-five, to be exact," Edwin cut in.

Jax and Ford shared a moment. Ford knew Jax had that information down to the ounce. He was just being a smart-ass.

"Where's your name?" Petie asked, squinting at the miniscule engraving.

Ford pointed to where his name had been etched along with the rest of the team and the coaches. He loved how the league handled it—not a replacement trophy each year for the winning team and not leaving it at just the team name. Everyone got a piece and it stayed that way until the band filled up. Sixty-five teams could fit on the Cup and the Rajuns' band wouldn't be removed until they'd run out of room. A lot of years left for his name to shine, and after that the strip would be placed in the Hockey Hall of Fame.

Immortality.

Ford slid a glance to his brother who was studying the engraving. Was he wishing that *F* was a *J*? Wishing *F* would eff himself? This had to be killing him.

Jax finally looked up, his eyes soft before they flattened. "Thanks for doing this."

Ford heard an apology in there, and it was good enough. He didn't want to spend his last couple days in Chicago fighting with his brother. Paulie wouldn't have wanted it this way. They had to make peace, even if it was stilted.

"Gotta have some perks, right?"

Coach put his head around the door. "Not gonna be able to keep them out for much longer, Fordie."

Ford looked at Edwin. "You ready, chief?"

Edwin waved in resignation. "So it begins."

ADDISON SANK below the bubble-laden surface of the tub in Harper's guest bathroom, relaxing for the first time that day. She'd been running around like a headless hen trying to get her ducks in a row for her move into her new loft apartment in the West Loop. This city was going to work for her. Big and bold and brash, just like Addison herself. Having a friend like Harper to smooth her entrance into the social circles would make all the difference.

And then there was Harper as Miss Matchmaker.

Addison chuckled to herself, thinking of that gleam in her friend's eye when she proposed creating a list of eligible men. Suitable men.

Men not like Ford Callaghan.

Bye-bye, happy place.

She shouldn't have given him her number. Not because it was a terrible idea for them to be in contact—which it was—or because the sizzling chemistry between them could go nowhere—which it couldn't—but because eighteen hours had passed and he hadn't used it.

The pain in his eyes when she opened the front door last night had cut her in half. And then the way he'd plowed into her body as if he wanted to split her in half had pretty much done her in. His mastery of her was a thing of beauty, but it was a beauty that could turn ugly very quickly. She thought she'd done the right thing—the mature thing—in offering to be his shoulder and even if he had to be all close-mouthed typical male about it, she'd hoped he would get in touch just to . . . get in touch.

A night and day later, and nothing.

Annoyed at her weakness and no longer able to enjoy this so-called relaxing bath, she pulled the plug, clambered out, and dried off. This was for the best. No good could come of it anyway. He was too young, too hot, too off limits.

Out of my mind you go, Ford Callaghan. Gracias for all the orgasms.

Her ears perked up like a lioness sensing danger on the savanna. What was that? Oh, hell. Exiting the bathroom, she almost broke her ankle sprinting to catch her ringing phone.

Missed call. She didn't recognize it and it could be anyone. She wouldn't usually answer an unknown number, except it might be . . .

It rang again.

"Hello?"

"Hey."

Thank God.

That voice like dark, decadent chocolate seeped into her bones, warming her more than the steaming water she'd just left. She sank down onto the bed, pulling at her towel nervously.

"Hey," she said back, sort of sharpish because she felt foolish at how ridiculously relieved she was to hear his voice.

"Sorry I didn't call sooner. It was my day with the Cup and I had a thing."

Of course. She'd read that last night and it completely flew from her brain.

"How'd it go?"

"Good. I took it to my old junior club so there were a lot of kids with their parents. My nephews as well. They went wild for it."

She laughed. "I bet. They must be your biggest fans."

"I don't know about that. They like the merch, for sure."

"So your family lives in Chicago?" She knew this already, but now it struck her strange he was staying in a hotel.

"Yeah, I'm staying with them now. It's . . . been a while since I've seen my brother. Been a while since I've been home."

So much meaning laden in that word. *Home.* Her heart checked, remembering what she'd learned about his past. That sorrow still hung over him like a heavy cloak. "Away games don't count," she said in sympathy.

"No, they don't."

She lay back on the bed, adjusting the phone to her ear. "He must be proud of you. Your brother."

Long pause. "He is. Well, I guess he is. It's just not how we imagined it would turn out."

"I read about Paul. I'm so sorry, Ford."

"Thanks, sweetheart. It was a long time ago, but thanks all the same." He waited a beat. Then another. She let him get there on his own schedule. "Things with my brother have been a bit strained."

"Since the accident?"

"Yep."

Ten years. This poor family, how they must have suffered. "Are your parents still around?"

"No. My dad died of cancer about six years ago, and my

mom didn't last much longer after that. Paulie's death really took it out of her. He wasn't supposed to go like that."

No one is. In those words, she heard the guilt he carried with him. She longed to throw her arms around him, console him with her body. But there could be no more of that. Giving him her number was purely so he could use her metaphorical shoulder, not her actual breasts, for comfort.

Ford's messy hair brushing against her breasts . . . *Focus, Addison.*

"Tell me about your brother, the one who lives in Chicago."

"Jax? He's so talented." He paused. "Well, he was. A wall of badass, nothing got by him. But quicker than someone his size should have been. He wasn't the same after the accident." *Because of me,* he may as well have said. All those regrets and *if onlys.*

"You were so young, Ford. Just a kid."

"Old enough. I was responsible for them. For getting them home safe. For making sure Paulie got to Toronto. Fuck—" He broke off, his memories overtaking his speech and sending it into a stall.

She sat up, her heart aching at his pain. What she would do to try to ease it if they were in the same room. "Baby, I'm here."

He huffed a laugh. It sounded rusty. "I didn't call to get all maudlin, y'know."

"No? Why did you call?"

"I could say I wanted to know what you were wearing but I think we've moved past that, don't you?"

She chuckled. "Probably." It felt like they'd leapfrogged all the steps and landed right in the comfort zone. How had that happened? "So, if you're not interested in this itty-bitty-little towel that's barely hanging on"—at his groan, she giggled evilly—"and you don't want to confide all your problems, then what's on your mind, Callaghan?"

"I'd like to see you again."

Ah. That's what she'd been hoping and dreading in equal measure.

"You know we can't. You know it's a terrible idea."

"So you say."

She thought about that, probably for too long because he spoke again.

"My family's throwing a party for me tonight at Jimmy's Tap in Bridgeport. Any chance you could stop by?"

A public event with people taking photos and uploading them to social media? Was he out of his Cup-winning mind?

"You know what I just said about this being a terrible idea. That goes double for public meetups in bars. Besides, that's not what's going on here, is it? This was never supposed to be anything more than—"

"Screwing in secret?"

"Right." That shouldn't have hurt her heart the way it did. She had "met" him three days ago and she sure as hell wasn't interested in anything more. Likely, her feminine pride was wounded because he had reduced it to its basest elements.

Pick a lane, Williams.

"I should go or my hair will dry into a bird's nest. So . . . good luck, Callaghan."

She heard his long intake of breath, a build to something more. But all he said was "Take care, sweetheart," and ended the call, leaving her chilled—and not from the damp towel wrapping her body either.

9

JIMMY'S TAP in Bridgeport was the kind of place a classy woman like Addison Williams wouldn't be seen dead in, so it was probably good she had turned down Ford's offer. It did, however, have all the elements of a great South Side dive bar: draft Pabst, decent Italian beef next door, and TVs switched to the White Sox game. Even in hockey and football season, Jimmy preferred to play reruns of the Sox winning the series in '05. (Cubbies? What Cubbies.)

No one dared to fuck with the remote.

At least that was the SOP in years gone by. Walking in, Jax had told Ford that Jimmy made an exception for the Rajuns going all the way because he was that proud of a local boy making good.

Another change since the last time Ford had was here was the addition of a patio. And as Ford was 99.9% certain that Jimmy didn't offer much in the way of party catering, he assumed Marcy must have put the whole hood on sandwich-making duty. He was equally sure that this much potato salad would never again be gathered in one spot. Must have cost a few Bennies. He'd slip her some cash later.

In Skates Trouble

"Pretty fancy patio, Jimmy," Ford said when the grizzled old-timer put his head outside. The guy was squinting like he worried his skin might burn from exposure to the elements. Ford couldn't recall ever seeing him in natural sunlight.

"Da kids seem to like it. Next dey'll be wantin' service at da fuckin' tables."

Now that was the Jimmy Ford knew and loved.

"Ya did good, Callaghan," Jimmy continued out of the side of his mouth, a mighty fine impression of Burgess Meredith in Rocky, "even if it was with da wrong team. Rebels shoulda picked you up when dey had a chance."

Three years ago, they'd tried to acquire him. Now, they couldn't afford him, not with the way he'd played during the series. He was a winner, a god among men, and any woman would be happy to have him.

Any woman but Addison.

Coming in tonight, he'd promised himself he wouldn't think of her, but the woman had a foothold in his brain, which was so not good for his mental well-being. She wasn't interested and why the hell would she be? Apart from the obvious complication with her ex, a jock was probably the last guy she'd want warming her bed. Guys like that accountant at Harper's dinner party were more her speed, even if he had been a condescending asshole with his "my wife won't need to work" bullshit.

He redirected his focus back to the party. Everyone and his aunt had detached from their sofas to celebrate with him, and it was a blast to see guys he'd gone to school with, girls he'd felt up behind the gym, and even his tenth grade math teacher, Mr. O'Brien, who now assured him he'd always known Ford "would go far." The same teacher who would flick a ruler at his ear because Ford liked to nap on his desk in the early afternoon. When you're up at 4:30 a.m. daily for hockey practice, sleep is more important than algebra.

The setting July sun cast a burnished glow over the Cup, now taking pride of place in the corner of the patio. Standing sentry, Edwin gave the evil eye to anyone who tried to lift it, but Ford was happy to let everyone touch it. The neighborhood was as responsible for taking him all the way as his parents, his brothers, and every coach who'd told him to haul ass down the other end of the rink and be quick about it. Let them enjoy this moment.

Jax took a seat beside Ford. They hadn't discussed the fight last night, but then, along with the non-hugging thing, there was also the non-talking thing. At least, not about anything important.

Ford opened with, "Thanks for putting this together."

"Thank Marcy," Jax gruffed out. Seeming to realize that this made him sound like more of an asshole than usual, he added, "Everyone's proud of you, Fordie."

Surprised as all hell, Ford turned to him, but his brother's focus was elsewhere. Jax's mouth had dropped open and he was staring at some spot over Ford's shoulder.

"Fuck me if that isn't Harper Chase."

Ford's head whipped around to take in the Chicago Rebels VP and would-be owner striding through the crowd toward their table. Panic scrambled his blood. Had something happened to Addy? Why the hell else would Harper be here?

He stood, which is when he realized that Harper was not alone. Two steps behind her, Addy appeared like a dying man's mirage in a sleeveless green blouse that matched her eyes and that did nothing to hide her assets. She didn't just

In Skates Trouble 81

walk; she owned every step, and as she drew closer, she
caught his eye and . . . holy shit, winked.

"Ford!" Harper said like she was greeting an old friend.
She leaned up on her tiptoes because even in heels she
barely came up to his pecs, and aimed a kiss that landed
somewhere near the underside of his chin. "Sorry I'm late.
When you said it was hard to find, you weren't kidding."

Okay.

"No worries, glad you could make it," he said, playing
along. That's right, no flies on him. He turned to his brother
who was watching with avid interest. "Harper, this is my
brother, Jackson Callaghan."

"Pleasure, Mr. Callaghan." Harper shook Jax's hand as
he stood. "And this is Addison. I hope you don't mind I
brought a gal pal. Safety in numbers as I venture into the
wilds of the South Side."

Ford nodded at Addy, knowing he should shake her hand
but also knowing that if he touched her, he'd likely cleave
her to his body and never let go. This had to be her idea and,
for some reason, Harper was playing fairy godmother. Why?

Bypassing him, Addy reached over and offered her hand
to Jax, who took it then raised an unsubtle eyebrow of "do
you know who the hell that is?" at Ford.

No one spoke for a good ten seconds.

Jax frowned, then swung his head back in Harper's
direction. "Come to see what a Cup celebration looks like,
Ms. Chase? Might be the closest you get."

Ford shot him a glare, but Harper had probably heard a
lot worse, given how badly the Rebels had performed this
past season. Last in pretty much every league metric. If they
were a British soccer team they would have been relegated
ten times over.

Harper's gaze strayed to the Cup, unmistakable envy in it. "No one gave the Rage much of a shot this year and now look at them. It's amazing what can be overcome if you want it enough." She dropped those last words on Ford, the implication as clear as Addy's glittering eyes.

If he wanted this woman, he was going to have to fight.

Torn between questioning why Harper Chase was on his side in this and pondering his next move, he almost missed Harper's breathy gush of, "So what are the chances of getting a martini?"

Jax looked amused. "Martinis would be about as likely as the Rebels winning the Cup next year, but I'm happy to escort you to our finest keg, Ms. Chase." He stood and led the way.

"Now be good while I'm gone, children." She cocked an eyebrow—yeah, real smart-ass, this one—and followed Jax into the crowd, leaving Ford alone with Addy. Or as alone as you could get in the middle of a South Side bar patio during a Cup celebration in your honor.

Ford allowed himself the luxury of taking inventory of this heart-stoppingly beautiful woman. She wore jeans that hugged every delicious curve like they were afraid to let go. Through the blouse, he could make out the swell of her breasts, the ones he'd had in his mouth less than twenty-four hours ago. Hours spent in a hell of craving, if he was being honest.

"You're staring," she murmured.

"You're stunning."

A fiery blush hit her cheeks. Who'd have expected a woman lauded right, left, and center for her looks would be embarrassed by a compliment? He liked that he could make her bloom like that.

"Would you like to sit?" he asked politely, praying she'd

say yes, because sitting was the only thing that would stop him from embarrassing himself. His jeans were not loose enough for this. Mercifully, she took his seat while he moved over to the one vacated by Jax.

"You probably have questions," she said.

"Only one."

Her teeth snagged on her lower lip. So not helping his boner.

He leaned in, inhaling what he could of her scent. Memorizing it for later. "Tell me, Bright Eyes. Are you a Cubs or a White Sox fan?"

She laughed, then covered her mouth with a guilty look at the crowd now latching on to her presence. "I'm a Yankees fan."

He closed his eyes. "Knew there was a reason this could never work." When he opened them again, he met a knowing gaze and a smile that slayed him.

Her smile faded. "I don't want to make trouble for you. I just couldn't leave our conversation the way it ended."

So this was goodbye. He had no idea which was worse: not seeing her again as he'd expected when he hung up the phone two hours ago or having her beside him in a state of frustrating untouchability.

Judging by the level of interest raised by her arrival, Ford had no doubt plenty of snaps were already clogging up Instagram and Twitter. The cover story should hold up: Michael Babineaux's ex-wife was here with Harper Chase, an acquaintance of Ford's. Two degrees of perfectly inno-cent separation.

Though they both knew it was nothing of the kind.

That's when something struck him like a slap shot to the head: Ford didn't care. Or rather, he cared about something else more. Someone else. Addy. She was a contradiction in so many ways. Externally she was beautiful—*stunning*—strong, self-sufficient, and driven to succeed. But he'd heard her voice on the balcony and at Harper's home. The vulnerability in it, masking a heart and soul that needed someone to back her. Cherish her. He wanted to be that someone.

He wanted to see her again and to hell with what people thought.

But it mattered to her, and that was the barrier he had to hurdle. "You could have called. Texted. You didn't have to come in person."

She hitched an eyebrow. "I was raised to do things properly. Not to take the coward's way out."

"And this afternoon, you were feeling cowardly? Or maybe just afraid?"

She smiled at the distinction he'd made. "All my life I've been told I didn't have it in me to succeed. I was too big, too curvy, too fat. I wasn't smart enough to do anything other than modeling, or I was too smart to get far in this business. I could be three times as rich if I lost thirty pounds, five times if I lost fifty." She waved a hand, her annoyance at the haters clear. "What I'm trying to say is that I've worked my famous ass off to get where I am. I know you've worked hard, too." She glanced around, her assessing gaze landing on Jax who was chewing Harper's ear off. Probably telling her how to fix the Rebels' defense.

"I have," he said cautiously, because he could hear the *but* in there, one he didn't want to deal with.

"We're attracted to each other. Off-the-charts attracted," she said, her voice low and husky and intoxicating. "I'm adult enough to admit that. But I'm also adult enough to know that this can't go anywhere, Ford. In fact, it's already gone too far. We've had our fun and anything more wouldn't be fun. It would be weighed down with worry and regret and drama. It would be hard, and I'm finished with hard when it comes to men."

He rolled his lips in and tried to react like an adult to the "hard" comment.

"Oh, shut it," she said good-naturedly, then more seriously, "neither am I looking for a relationship and if I was—"

"It wouldn't be with a bruiser like me."

She rolled her eyes. "Less of the self-pity, Callaghan. It wouldn't be with a man whose career would be destroyed by an association with me. This is impossible."

Impossible was just an opinion. Damn, every word out of her mouth only made him want her more, which was so fucking perverse considering the BS coming out of that gorgeous mouth.

A couple people eyed them with interest. It was already starting, and he checked in with his brain to see if that was okay. The noodle shot back with: *No complaints here.* Addy just needed a chance to get used to the idea.

"Don't shut us down just yet. Think on it for a little while. If you still feel the same way in a day or two, then I'll respect your wishes. But don't dismiss the possibilities without giving your brain a chance to engage."

"So if I'm thinking of you while you're not around, there's something more to this than just lust?"

"A couple of days out of my orbit and you'll be begging me to hit that gorgeous ass and then make you a sandwich." He broke out his widest, panty-dropping grin. "And Addy, let me tell you, my post-coital sandwiches are legendary."

"This was a mistake."

Addison sipped her beer and eyed Harper as if this was all her fault. Harper, knowing Addison well, took it in the spirit intended.

"You wanted to see him again and—oh, right. That's it." She swirled her beer around a plastic cup, evident distaste in the motion. Harper was not a beer girl, which was sort of strange for a woman who lived and breathed hockey. "So you could assure yourself there's nothing worth pursuing when even I could have told you that Killer Callaghan's ass is most definitely worth pursuing. The guy's as hot as puck."

Hockey humor. Hilarious.

"He sounded so disappointed when I said I wouldn't stop by." Which is when she had proposed that Harper show up at the party to wish him well, being a fellow hockey professional, and *hey boys, look who I brought. A lingerie supermodel. You're welcome!*

"I so hate letting people down," Addison added unnecessarily.

"Which is why you stayed married two years and eight months longer than you should have. Oh, God, I can't take this anymore." She tapped the shoulder of an older gentleman who was picking up Solo cups and trashing them in a plastic bag attached to his wrist. "Young man, would you be so kind as to make me a dirty martini with three olives?"

The "young man" who didn't look a day under eighty twisted his mouth in a sneer.

"Anything for a lady." Amazingly, not said with sarcasm. That was just the natural set of his mouth.

"Jimmy, you are a lifesaver," Harper said with a cheeky grin.

They knew each other?

He smiled, revealing a toothy gap. "Been a while, Harper. How's that old fart you call a father?"

Harper smiled sweetly, though Addison saw tungsten in that grin. She and her dad had a tricky relationship, to say the least. "Not quite as ornery as you. So tell me, Jimmy, how're the kids?"

Two minutes later, they'd learned all about Jimmy's four kids, ten grandchildren, and one ingrate of a son-in-law. When he moved off to make Harper's martini, she turned back to Addison.

"Where were we? Oh, yes. You fucked this boy on a Persian carpet yesterday, and today you're wondering if the chemistry between you can be dismissed out of hand. You might be all caught in his sex-ray, but—"

"But?"

"That boy is a little bit crazy for you, and I think you're a little bit gaga for him. I'm not sure if that's good or bad, but it definitely is a fact. He hasn't taken his eyes off you the entire time you've been here."

This was true. They'd spent only a few moments together before he was whisked away for photos. Definitely a good thing, because she'd been this close to feeling him up beneath the table.

His utter self-confidence that she wouldn't be able to stay away from him floored her. Of course he was right—she was here, wasn't she?—but she didn't have to enjoy that he was right, nor that he was so cocky with it.

Though that wasn't quite it. Ford's assurance didn't stem from arrogant conceit like her husband had excelled in, but from a comfort with who he was. Unlike Michael, Ford was respectful. Of her. Of *them*.

More accustomed to guys who focused on her figure, for both positive and negative reasons, Addy didn't have a lot of experience with men seeing beyond the image to the woman beneath. The woman with goals and dreams and needs—both emotional *and* physical.

And right now, those physical needs were getting her into all sorts of trouble as her damn nipples headed out on a search mission. Ford stood near the Cup, his Viking warrior beauty reflected in it while he explained something to three young boys—his nephews, she guessed from the resemblance. Clearly, he was crazy about them and they adored him in spades. He threw back his head, laughing at something the shortest one said, and the vision of his tan throat got a ten from the nipple judges.

We have gone zero days without a panties-dampening episode.

His gaze clashed with hers, and she let it linger for a few dangerously long seconds. Was that it? The thrill of playing footsie with taboo? She wasn't the daredevil sort, but something about Ford brought out this crazy, wild version of her.

On a balcony, in a bathroom . . . on a Persian rug, for crying out loud.

"Here you go, Harper." Jimmy had returned with what looked like a perfectly made martini for Harper, complete with three olives.

"A martini in Jimmy's Tap?" Harper mused as she accepted the glass. "And they said it couldn't be done. Maybe a Rebels run at the Cup is more likely than people think." The mention of the Rebels' martini-in-a-dive chances of success inspired the Tap's owner to launch into a spirited deconstruction of the team's failure of a season. The price paid for a decent cocktail, Addison supposed.

Her phone buzzed in her purse. She took it out.

Ford: *Meet me inside the bar.*

Hell, no. A common-sense infusion was needed. *Now.*

Taking advantage of Harper's distraction, Addison texted back: *That sounds like a bad idea.*

Ford: *Just for a minute.*

Breathing deeply, she looked up—then wished she hadn't. Ford had locked eyes with her, his face tight with hunger, his intent clear. That lava gaze found a corresponding callback in her body, an undeniable beat that thrummed stronger with each passing second.

She wanted him. She had never wanted anyone or anything this much.

Harper and Jimmy were chatting and everyone else was busy. They wouldn't be missed, surely. Just a moment. Just a moment to touch.

Addison: *One minute.*

One last time, she told herself. Then she would hop on the train for sanity.

10

THIS WAS CUCKOO. Absolutely nuts.

Yet Ford couldn't help himself. It was if he was in some sort of fuck-trance, a pheromone fog whenever Addy was near.

The only people in the bar were a couple of old timers watching the Sox getting their asses handed to them by the Royals. Addy stood near the short end of the L-shaped bar, checking her phone. Through the honey-brown veil of her lashes, she watched as he approached.

"Ford, I just came in here to tell you that we can't—"

Ignoring that because he suspected the end of the sentence wouldn't be conducive to the raging erection that needed attention, he took her hand and led her down the corridor to the back office. Inside he dragged her, shut the door, and kissed her like his life depended on it.

Right now, it felt like it truly did.

He had to convince her, and he worried that even giving her time to think about it might not result in the W.

"Ford, what are you—oh fuck it, I know exactly what you're doing, you tricky bastard." She pushed at his shoulders, separating their lips. Absolute hell. "You're *supposed* to be giving my brain a chance to come around to your attractions."

"How's that working out?"

"My brain is the one organ who is not on your side right now. But everything else . . ."

"I'm liking how everything else is thinking." He kissed her again, pouring all his hunger into it, every ounce of need. But he knew he'd been pushing her in a big way, using the hormone overload to direct traffic. If she wanted this— whatever *this* was—he needed to hear it from her.

Pulling back was the hardest thing he'd ever done.

He stepped away from heaven and took a seat in Jimmy's chair. His cock punched hard against his zipper but he told it to behave.

"That first night at the hotel, I imagined licking you to completion as I jacked off. I could feel the imprint of your clit on my tongue, taste your honey on my lips."

He watched how her breasts heaved and her thighs squeezed together.

"Since then, I've been inside you, felt you like a vise around my dick. I've tongued your nipples, inhaled your scent. But I still haven't drunk you down properly. That's what I want right now. That's what I want you to give me."

Her breath came in short tugs, hitches in her chest that moved her breasts beautifully. "You can—you can just take it."

"All I've done so far is take. I've been maneuvering you into rooms, kicking down doors, persuading you to let me in. I want this to be mutual."

She laughed, a nervous tinkle. "You'd think I'd do this if I didn't want to?"

"I think it's easy to get caught up in the moment. Caught

up in us. I want you to decide, Addy." He realized he was setting some kind of test of her willingness to take the next step, not just in this small office but maybe tomorrow or the day after that.

He hadn't intended to push, but he wasn't a fling kind of guy. Two facts were clear to him: one, he wanted more, and two, he didn't want to sneak around. He recognized it might take a little longer to get her into that mindset but he'd take a sign of it here and now.

"Puck's in your half, Addy."

Maybe a hockey reference was a touch too close for home because that threw her. Scowling beautifully, she straightened against the door, determination in her body language that signaled she might be thinking of leaving.

Or coming closer.

She reached behind her and locked the door, then took a step toward him. And another.

His cock stiffened to the point he wouldn't be surprised to find his zipper imprinted on it later.

Less than a foot of space separated them. He gripped the chair's armrests so he wouldn't reach out and close the gap between them.

This was her distance to erase.

Her fingers, polish-topped with a sparkly pink, unsnapped her jeans and drew her zipper down, all while she held his gaze with a carnal gleam in her own. He saw power in it and it made him proud to be her man.

No doubt about it. Ford Callaghan was owned by this woman.

She pushed her jeans down, leaving a virginal-white, lace-trimmed triangle. The dark strip of hair shadowing it made his mouth water.

He expected she'd move closer, offer her body to his

thirsty mouth, but she surprised him by turning. She wiggled out of her jeans, her perfect ass swaying before him like a hypnotist's pendulum. A spaghetti-thin strap of white bisected her glorious cheeks, a small patch of lace above the cleft like a target his eyes—and soon his tongue—should take aim at.

Kicking off the jeans, she placed her palms on Jimmy's desk, her famous booty showcased like a glorious sculpture that wouldn't look out of place in some museum. It wasn't his imagination that she rubbed her thighs together as she did it, clearly seeking relief. He stroked a hand over his erection in sympathy.

"Take it, Ford. Take what I'm giving you."

Jesus H. What had he unleashed?

The scrape of the chair's wheels as he scooted over sounded loud, but his groan on getting up close and scenting her arousal had it beat for decibels. She was a big girl, no denying it, and there was nothing sexier than how she owned it.

His first touch of his fingertips to her skin found her trembling. Slowly, he dragged her panties down because despite how pretty they were, he needed unrestricted access. Nothing would get in the way of his tongue.

As if she sensed his need, she raised a knee onto the desk, displaying for him the sweetest sight he'd ever laid eyes on. Pretty in pink, glistening like a jewel, she was already moaning in anticipation. Just as his mouth was already watering for the same reason.

"I lick this, it's mine." Better she be warned.

He waited for her acquiescence, needing that final word.

"Yes."

Inclining his head, he indulged in one long, delicious stroke of his tongue through her.

"Ford, oh, God." She hitched her ass up higher, shoving it closer, making her need evident. "More. Don't stop. Please."

He spread her cheeks apart and slipped his thumbs in, separating. Her slick arousal dripped on his hands, so never one to be wasteful, he scooped all that honey up with this tongue.

Her taste. Sweet, tangy, best he'd ever had, bar none. He stroked a finger through, giving her swollen clit a testing swipe. She bucked in pleasure. He did it again, and then he applied his mouth to eating this woman out so she would never want another man's tongue within a five-mile radius of her body. He would convince her that pleasure like this was worth taking a risk on.

That *they* were worth taking a risk on.

For the longest time, he'd questioned whether he deserved to feel this good. This hopeful. He had wealth, talent, now the Cup, but it was nothing without someone to share it. He saw that same need in Addy—her drive, her push to succeed against the odds. Against the judgment.

He continued, teasing, tasting, devouring, layering sensation upon sensation, until she finally shattered against his mouth. Yeah. The physical risk was definitely worth the reward.

Now he just had to convince her of the rest.

Ford watched as Addy redressed.

"A gentleman would turn his back."

He canted his head like he was taking in a *Playboy* centerfold. "Just savoring for my memory banks. And this gentleman plans to put eating out Addison Williams as a marketable skill on his résumé."

She giggled and shook her head. "Wow, eavesdropping does pay. You *do* know what women want."

He stood and gathered her in his arms. "I know what this woman wants. And I know what I want and what I can give you." He kissed her softly. "After that great demonstration of my talents, are you gonna tell me I'm not up for the job of being your man?"

Her eyes turned glassy, a mix of desire and need. Apprehension, too. "You said you'd give me time away from you to think about it? Ten minutes after that promise, your face is between my thighs."

"Just trying to help you come to the right decision," he said with a grin, then gravely, "give us a chance, Addy."

She pushed him away. Gently, but it was still a push. "Sneaking around so we don't upset my ex-husband?"

"So, he's still crazy about you then? Can't blame him." But hell if he had to like it.

"He's not. He just doesn't like to lose." Her brow furrowed. "We weren't all that compatible and he liked to make decisions for me. What to wear. What jobs to take. A little like what you're trying to do now. Sex is one thing, dating is a whole other hockey game."

"So if your ex wasn't my boss, you'd have no problems moving this forward?"

"I wouldn't say that, exactly."

He crowded her against the door of the office. "What would you say? Exactly?"

She screwed her nose up. Cute as hell. "You're younger than me. Much younger."

"And you need a younger man to keep you satisfied, Addy." He let his hand coast to the round of her beautiful ass and cupped it like it belonged to him. "You're filled with passion and ambition and appetites, and I'm the man to match you. I want a woman who knows who she is, who doesn't need me to define her because she's already her own person. My age, your ex, those facts are meaningless in the face of what we've started here. I think we could be pretty amazing together, Addison Williams."

Her bottom lip wobbled and she closed her eyes, absorbing his words. Into her heart, he hoped, because that was his target. He needed her to know that he planned to fight for her.

When she opened them again, he saw she was still trying to hold her ground, though he'd blown a hole in one barrier to her resistance. So, she needed time to come around. He'd made his case. He'd give her space.

But not for long.

Giving Addy the time she needed to return to the patio, Ford leaned on the bar and watched the slight wobble to her gait with satisfaction.

"Are you out of your fucking mind?"

Ford turned to catch Jax thumbing over his shoulder at Addison's departing back. Her lips were kiss-stung, her skin was flushed, and even a blind man could deduce something intensely physical and raw had just occurred between them.

"None of your business, Jax."

His brother's face turned as dark as the sticky bar floor they could barely see. He pushed Ford back down the corridor.

"None of my business? You're screwing your boss's woman."

In Skates Trouble   97

"She's not his woman. Not anymore. They've been divorced for nearly two years."

"I'm sure that's going to be a real consolation when he sees the two of you together. Because he will find out. Unless this is just a one-off."

Ford swallowed, that phrase booming through his skull. One-off? Hell, no. He would make this happen.

It didn't take long for Jax to figure that out for himself. He fisted Ford's T-shirt and pushed him back so hard Ford's head hit a framed photo. He thought it might be the one of Jimmy with The Big Hurt, Frank Thomas.

"You're going to see her again? Are you out of your tree? He'll make you pay."

Maybe. Maybe not. "He can't fire me. He has no legal grounds to do it."

"Doesn't need to fire you, asshole. He can trade you to some piece-of-shit team, or worse, he'll keep you benched for the whole of next season. You might never play again but whatever, it'll give you plenty of energy to fuck his whore."

A red haze darkened Ford's vision at the edges, and he did the one thing that had been coming for a long time now: he took a swing at his brother. Not really fair because Ford had thirty pounds on Jax and was in a hundred times better shape. But no one spoke about his woman that way.

Jax managed to stay upright, even as he staggered back, his hand to his jaw.

"You prick. You're going to destroy everything we built." Instead of anger in his brother's voice, Ford heard nothing but sorrow. "We placed all our hopes on you, Fordie. You were the only one left, carrying all the dreams forward. And now you want to mess with all that for a woman."

He knew it was crazy but, yes. Addison was the kind of woman men went to bat for. Risked careers for. Fought wars over. His life was hockey but he could also have this. He just had to be a man about it.

Ford stared at the brother he had just punched, searching for remorse that refused to come. For ten years, guilt and recrimination had been his constant companions. No more.

"I can't do this anymore, Jax. I can't carry this weight you've loaded on me since that night. I screwed up but you shouldn't have put me in that position either. Both of you so fuckin' drunk that a dumb kid with his learner's permit was left holding the bag."

He should have called a cab, his parents, anyone. But Paulie shoved the keys in his hand and told him, "*Don't be a pussy, Fordie. It's only a few fucking rain drops.*"

Jax's mouth twisted in anger. "It was an accident. No one blames you."

"You fucking liar. You've been blaming me for ten years. For your leg, for your life, for the void left when he died. Do you ever think that maybe some of the responsibility for what happened lay at your feet? You and Paulie both? You were supposed to take care of me, Jax. You were older, and you were supposed to look out for me but you didn't, brother. You let me drive that car in pounding rain. You let me kill him."

"Fordie." Jax's face crumpled, his eyes wide with shock. Did he think it was easy achieving a dream when his own brother resented every ice-eating stride? Did he understand for a second how alone he'd felt these last ten years?

Ford curled a hand around his brother's neck, the closest they'd been to each other since that night of celebratory joy when they'd given each other sloppy hugs coming out of the bar. "You don't know how many times I've wanted to give up. Pack it in. Lie down dead. With every ticket in your name left begging at the pick-up window, I wondered how I could go on."

Jax visibly swallowed. "You do it for Paulie."

He'd thought that once. He'd thought he was doing it for both of them.

"No, Jax, I do it for myself. Yeah, you might have been the hard-ass getting my lazy butt out of bed every morning for practice, and I might have grumbled at you and loved you all the same. But since that night, you've not been a brother to me. You've not given me a single sign that you're proud. When you said it tonight, I almost believed it, but I think you're just reciting it rote to make Marcy happy. Keep the peace. I don't think you'll ever see me the way you used to. Your little bro who had to train ten times as hard to keep up with you. Yeah, it should have been Paulie or you holding that Cup, but it's not. It's me, and I worked hard to get it."

His brother was shaking, whether from anger or something else, Ford neither knew or cared. He'd yearned for his brother's pride for so long, but now? Now it wasn't what he wanted or needed.

"And you could have more," Jax said, his voice a gutted rasp. "More Cups, more records, more glory. You wanna throw it all away for a piece of tail?"

"If I do, I sure as hell won't be thinking of you or Paulie when I do it. I won that Cup fair and square. It's mine. Just like Addy is."

He released Jax, who slumped against the wall behind him in the narrow corridor, all fight gone. And Ford walked away, thinking he'd just made a bad analogy.

He might have won the Cup but it was only his for a day. He planned to hold on to Addy for longer than that.

11

ADDISON STOOD in the center of her living room, hands clenched on hips, her eyes greedily taking it all in. Boxes needed to be opened, pictures needed to be hung, and champagne needed to be uncorked—and then guzzled in celebration.

She was finally in her new home in Chicago, and tomorrow, she would check in on how the ad campaign for *Beautiful* by Addison was coming along. T & A shouldn't be difficult to market, but she was in this business for more than the hard sell. She was promoting hope and possibility to women who didn't always think they deserved to feel attractive. Sexy was more than a pretty bra and panties. Sexy was the confidence to rock what you've got.

Sexy was a guy who locked eyes with you across a crowded bar patio and made you want more than you'd ever wanted in your life.

Her phone buzzed.

Speak of the chocolate-eyed devil . . .

Ford: *Hey.*

Addison studied the screen, marveling at how thinking

about him had conjured him out of the electronic ether. He was back in New Orleans, but they'd talked for several hours over the last week since the party at Jimmy's Tap. Movies, music, food. Their lives before that night on the balcony. So many details, like an old-fashioned courtship.

Those words he left with her—*I think we could be pretty amazing together*—still resonated in her blood and were spreading their tentacles into her heart and soul. Their sexual chemistry was undeniable, yet she was beginning to think in terms that didn't necessarily involve her hormones.

Or not just her hormones.

Perhaps they could keep it under wraps. He could visit when he had a few days between games. At least three times per season, he had to play the Chicago Rebels because they were part of the Western Conference. Their dirty little secret, their continued safety in the dark. It would be enough for her. It would have to be.

She refocused on his text message.

Hey? Typical man. God forbid he elaborate.

Addison: *Hey, yourself.*

Ford: *What are you not wearing?*

Addison: *Really?*

Ford: *Can do this all day.*

She laughed. Boy, she had missed him.

Addison: *I'd like to hear your voice.*

Seconds passed, each as long as an hour. *Stupid, Addison. Stupid, stupid.*

Ford: *Then open up.*

She blinked at the last message. Could he mean . . . ?

A knock on the door answered her question. The joy in her chest was really too much. *Tamp it down. Don't make a fool of yourself.*

She bounded to the door. *Less bounding, woman. Bounding is for dogs.*

Tearing the door open, she tried to school her expression to bland but his big, goofy smile was the first thing she saw and it made hers erupt all over her face.

"Hey, Bright—"

She was in his arms before he could finish, her mouth on his hot and hungry.

"I can't believe you're here," she gasped between blistering kisses. "I didn't expect you."

He hitched her up around his hips, no simple task given she was a big girl, but God, he made it seem so easy. He made *this* seem so easy.

"I had to see you," he murmured. *Hot kiss.* "Been thinking about you all week." *Hotter kiss.* "This okay?"

"Yes." *Hottest kiss of all.*

He pushed her against the hallway wall, leaving the door to her apartment open. "Couldn't wait. Had to have you."

Her yoga pants made it halfway down her thighs and her panties didn't even get that far. He just pushed them aside and pushed two fingers inside her.

"Addy," he groaned as if it was more of his body and not just those fingers.

She tore at his zipper, needing to free him, because she knew he was suffering. Already, she knew he needed to drive deep and she needed him to do it. So badly.

Desire was their default setting but his words were like a balm to her healing heart. *I had to see you. Been thinking about you all week.* They hadn't spent much time discussing who they were, what they wanted in life, whether they could really make it together, but there had been a quiet comfort with him from the moment they first spoke. *He heard her. He saw her.* Today, he came for her, and she had a feeling he always would.

A few times a year could never be enough.

Somehow, she'd fallen in love with a hockey player.

Afterward, they lay on the floor, panting back to normal, except in Addy's case, normal had to be recalibrated. An already tricky situation had just become a hundred times more complicated. She had fallen for this big, beautiful, made-her-feel-happy guy.

"I don't recall giving you my address, Callaghan."

"Haven't you heard? Harper Chase is a good pal of mine," he whispered against her ear.

"Do you think we might actually make it to a bed one of these days?"

"Clearly, our best work is done on rugs."

The door was still open. "One of my new neighbors could walk by any minute. Quite an introduction."

He nudged the door closed with his boot, but made no effort to move or cover himself. Baby Jesus in the manger, he was glorious, jutting proudly and still erect. She felt an urge to kiss him. So she did. Right on the still swollen, damp crown.

That's when it hit her.

"We didn't use a condom."

He blew out a breath. "Baby, I'm sorry. I just saw you and the next thing I know—"

"I was there, Callaghan." She scooted up and kissed him, long and luxurious on his lips. "I assume I have nothing to worry about."

"I promise."

She nodded. "And your lucrative contract is safe. No paternity claims in your future."

Something shadowed over his face, a discomfort she hadn't seen marring his handsomeness before. "Wouldn't be the worst thing to happen." He skimmed a hand over her belly, his previous unease now replaced by something that looked a lot like yearning. She knew she wanted children eventually, but Michael hadn't been interested. He had told her it would ruin her figure, which was rich considering he didn't want her to use that figure earning a living.

He merely wanted the benefits for himself.

Ford respected her and her ambitions. If it ever came to a point where they took this further, she knew they would work it out together. As a team. She had no reason for hope but it was here inside her, bursting to get out.

For now, she reined in those runaway thoughts.

"You hungry?" she asked.

"Starving. But like I promised before, after sex, I make the sandwiches."

ADDISON'S PHONE rang on the nightstand, cutting into a very pleasant dream about Ford taking her hard in the executive box at the Cajun Rage arena while he wore a Rebels jersey and nothing else. Weird, because he with the Rajuns. Clearly her mind was trying to remove all traces of her ex from her dream consciousness.

Struggling awake, she smiled, her body feeling well-used and pleasure-sated. Ford was here in the flesh, had shown up last night and stayed. This was madness, yet somehow she didn't have the willpower to throw him out.

She wanted this, wanted to see if they could carve a path out for this thing they were building together.

She ignored the phone, not ready for the reality intrusion. It rang again. Another ignore, then the buzz of a text. And again.

Someone *really* wanted her to answer. She checked the screen.

Harper: *We need to talk. Now.*

With a smile over her shoulder at the naked god tangled up in her sex-rumpled sheets, she sidled from the bed and walked outside the bedroom (okay, hobbled). Ford's résumé of marketable sex skills was getting longer and longer.

She called Harper back. "What's so urgent?"

"Is Ford with you?"

"Yep, he's sleeping off my use and abuse." She giggled, feeling silly. But happy. God, so happy.

"Michael knows."

All that happy turned to sludge in her gut. "How? We've been so careful. How could he—?"

"My contact at the Rajuns says it came from Callaghan himself. Ford walked into Michael's office yesterday and told him he wanted to date you."

The sludge rose to her chest, clumping into a bright ball of fury. "Are you kidding me? Why the hell would he do that?"

Harper sighed. "He's got it bad, babe. And he's prepared to risk his spot on the team to make this work."

"But, we hardly know each other. We've only just met and—" Her voice was climbing in panic. What the hell had he been thinking? He just waltzed in and told Michael? "What did your contact say? What happens now?"

"Michael is weighing his options. Nothing in Ford's contract forbids him from dating the ex-wife of the team's owner, but," she gave a slight, embarrassed cough, "I can't imagine Michael saying 'Hey ho, that's just swell, buddy. Bang away.'"

Neither could Addison.

But that wasn't what had her muscles itching to pop from her skin. Granted, the fact Michael now knew was not preferred but more important was *how* he knew. What in all that was holy was Ford thinking in fessing up? He had gone over her head and outed them. And there was only one reason he would have done it.

To force her hand.

Not cool. A dick move, actually. This was the kind of behavior she'd expect from her ex, a man with an ego as big as all outdoors. Michael was fond of the executive decision, of treating their marriage like an asset in his empire where he called all the shots. She'd never felt like a partner. Never felt like his equal. To find that Ford would think nothing of treating her with such disrespect ripped the air from her lungs.

"He had no right to make this decision without consulting me."

Harper's sigh was world-weary. "And there's that."

12

FORD EXTRACTED his ringing phone from his jeans, the ones that were halfway between the door and Addy's bed. That made him smile but then the sight of his agent's overly tanned face wiped the self-satisfaction clean off. Ford steeled himself for the inevitable fallout from his visit to Rajuns' HQ yesterday.

His mind went back to his meeting with Babineaux. Only the second time he'd been allowed to contaminate the owner's office with his presence and there was an excellent chance it would be his last. But he refused to sneak around like a kid on curfew.

Babineaux had stood up and rounded the desk, his hand outstretched.

"Callaghan, good to see you. Just back from Chicago, I hear. How'd it go?"

"Good." Ford gripped the boss's hand. "Saw family. Toured with the Cup. Plenty of nice media coverage."

Babineaux nodded approvingly and gestured at a leather seat. He leaned against the antique desk, his long legs in gray charcoal wool. He always wore a suit to the games and even now, he looked so put together that Ford doubted himself. If this was the kind of guy Addison liked then why the hell would she want anything to do with a lug like him?

But this man didn't make her happy, while Ford knew in his heart of hearts that he could. There was more than just sizzling sexual chemistry between them. The connection he felt with Addison was real and she felt it, too. Whatever barriers needed smashing, he would bring the dynamite. Starting now.

"What can I do for you, Callaghan? Not trying to negotiate for a bonus, are you?"

"I leave the dirty fighting to my agent," Ford replied. His agent was not going to appreciate that Ford had gone to Babineaux without looping him in, but this was personal, not business. "I need to run something by you. I met someone in Chicago."

Babineaux's brows rose, likely wondering why Ford's personal life warranted a cozy tête-à-tête.

"And you're telling me because?"

"I want to respect you by letting you know before you hear it from someone else." He inhaled a sharp breath. "It's Addison."

"What's Addison?"

"The person I met. Addison Williams."

Babineaux froze. His face, his body, the air around him.

"You're in a relationship with Addison?" Clipped, lethal.

"Not yet, but I want to be." Best to fudge that so the idea of Ford fucking the man's ex-wife didn't take root. At least, not immediately. "We met a few days ago and the attraction is there. She's reluctant to take it further."

"Why?"

Ford shrugged, though it locked up his shoulders instead of easing anything. "She's worried you'll retaliate. Against me." At least he hoped that was her primary concern.

Babineaux smirked. "And there I was thinking that maybe she was worried about hurting my feelings."

Pretty rich coming from the guy who had a different woman in the box every game. Maybe it was the classic gambit of hiding your pain in a haze of tail but that didn't seem likely given how Addy had described him. Babineaux just didn't enjoy losing. And that sure as hell wasn't reason enough for Ford to walk on eggshells around him.

"I suppose she's told you about me," the boss said, sounding mighty uncomfortable.

Ford shook his head. "Not a word. I don't need to know what happened between you. That's your business. I just want her to be able to move forward without any threats to either of us hanging over our heads."

That earned him a hard-nosed stare, no more than he expected. Ford was tired of living his life as an apology. He didn't owe Jax a career served out as if he was doing time. He didn't owe Michael Babineaux his balls served on a silver platter. The only person he owed was himself.

He wanted Addy. He wanted to see where this might go, and eliminating the obstacles up front was the best—the only—way to approach it.

"You took a risk coming here," Babineaux finally said after a ball-shriveling silence. "Damn gusty."

Ford heard admiration there, but he didn't think it would lead him out of the woods. Men like Babineaux didn't get to be men like Babineaux without playing a little hardball.

Ford merely nodded, preferring to let the boss lead. This was the trickiest part of the conversation. The moment held, suspended on the th-thunk of Ford's heartbeat.

Babineaux thrust out his hand. "I think we're done here."

Ford hauled his brain back to the present and the phone call he needed to deal with in the here and now.

"Hey, Tommy."

"Hey, Tommy?" his agent sputtered predictably. "*Hey, Tommy*? What the fuck is that? And what the hell are you doing having career-destroying chats with Michael Babineaux? Please tell me the rumors aren't true."

He played along. "The rumors aren't true."

"Thank God."

"They're not rumors. I'm seeing Addison, and Babineaux will just have to deal."

Tommy made a choking sound. "Just have to deal? Just. Have. To—"

"Man, you are going to have to stop repeating me. I *know* what I said. This is personal between Babineaux and me, and there's nothing here that concerns you."

"*Noth*—do you know what he's gonna do to you? You have two years left on your contract, and he'll make those two years hell. You'll be on the bench for most of it. You'll never play in the Finals again. And then when you're up for a trade, he'll send you to some shitty team like *the Rebels*. Is that what you want? The prime years of your career spent with your balls riding the pine or skating for a bunch of losers?"

A nagging discomfort came over him as he sat heavily on the bed. Sure, Babineaux could do that but the man would have to eventually see reason. Ford was a valued asset. Businessmen did not allow their personal feelings get in the way of making money, and Ford on the ice made money for the Rajuns. Besides, the fans would crucify a team owner who screwed with a star player's career because of masculine pride.

"I've got it under control."

"Glad you think so," he heard behind him.

He turned, and there she was, the woman of his dreams.

Except she didn't look nearly as happy to see him as she had last night.

"Later, Tommy." Ford hung up on his agent's unmanly squeal. "Hey, Bright Eyes."

"What the hell were you thinking?"

He didn't pretend to misunderstand her. "I'm not sneaking around, Addy. If we're going to do this, we're going to do it properly."

"So you made the unilateral decision to talk to my ex-husband about how you'd like to what—date me?"

Ford nodded. "Date you, be with you, make you mine."

She covered her face with her hands. "That is not your decision to make, Callaghan. I hardly know you. A week ago, you were a strange voice on a hotel balcony. Now you're discussing my dating future with my ex-husband."

Perhaps he should have given her a heads-up before he walked into Babineaux's office, but she would've tried to talk him out of it. The next step would've been her telling him that no fling was worth the threat to his career. And after that . . . it'd be *bye-bye, Callaghan.*

Starting as they meant to go on was the only way. Of this he was certain.

That didn't quite explain why he neglected to clue her in when he came over last night, but the second he'd seen her, all his blood had hurtled south. This was her fault, really, for being so damn gorgeous.

He kept that nugget to himself.

"Sweetheart, I had to do something. You know what's between us is crazy, strong, and real. I want to follow that to its logical conclusion."

"Logical? This isn't logic. Just sheer staking of territory. You may as well have peed on me." She rubbed her forehead. "What did he say?"

"He took it pretty well. Thanked me for being upfront."

She stopped in her fury-filled tracks, hands on hips. "And you believed him?"

No. He didn't. But that didn't change what was happening here. He and Addison were happening, and this passion needed to freight-train it all the way to the terminal.

"Addy, I don't know what kind of hold he has—or had over you. But what happens between you and me isn't for anyone else to decide."

"Except for you alone, apparently." Her eyes flew wide. "I can't do this. I can't be responsible for what happens when Michael turns on you. And believe me, he will. Neither will I stand by while you engage in some pissing contest with my ex."

He saw her fear in the pulse beating at the base of her throat, the one he'd licked and kissed last night. He knew what it was like to let fear mold your life. He also knew a thing or two about regrets.

He cupped her face with both hands. "I want you more than I've ever wanted anything. More than a professional hockey career. More than the Cup. This isn't going to go away because you're scared of the consequences. It's happened fast, but that doesn't make it any less valid. This need I have for you, Addy, is real. It's true."

"It's just sex, Callaghan." She jerked out of his grasp and started pacing up and down. She was scared, but she was also angry, and it was magnificent. "You're young and have probably been hit a few times too many against the boards. This isn't anything more. And it certainly isn't real or true."

One of them needed to be the brave one here. "Pretty sure it is, Addy."

She threw up her hands. "I just got out of a relationship—"

In Skates Trouble   113

"Eighteen months ago."

She didn't look too appreciative of his interruption. "I'm about to open a brand-new business and I do not have time for this. And that's before we get to all the other crap, such as you going behind my back to get my ex's permission to date me before you had mine. This is not the 1950s. I won't be another man's trophy, Ford."

That's what she thought? Hell, he already had a damn trophy. Had worked hard for it, and he would work equally hard for this. For her. He wanted this real, flesh-and-blood, passionate woman.

"I need you to take a leap, Addy. This is terrifying, I know, but it's what I want, and I'm pretty sure it's what you want."

"Don't be so sure you know what I want, Ford. Men have made that mistake before. Even if I wanted to date you, I'm not sure I can be with someone who so clearly thinks with his dick."

He grasped her hand and laid it over his chest, making sure she absorbed the vital beat beneath her soft palm. It thumped for her and her alone. "My heart, Addison Williams. This is a decision straight from the heart."

She looked woebegone, as if that was the worst thing he could have said. Had he misjudged this? Perhaps it was a little high-handed, but he wanted to remove the obstacles that stopped her from seeing a clear vista to the finish line.

She jerked her hand away. "I can't do this, Ford. There isn't enough here to justify these huge changes in your life. In my life."

"Are you denying you have feelings for me?"

She appeared to steel herself. "You're a nice boy, Ford. But you've got a lot to learn about relationships. I won't be held hostage to my hormones, and I won't be made to feel I owe you a shot because you did something incredibly dumb and disrespectful."

Nice boy? That's not what she was saying when she begged him to take her over and over last night. Dumb? So his Mensa application wouldn't pass muster. But disrespectful? Shit, he was trying to make this easier on her. On them both.

"So what was the plan, Addy? I sneak into Chicago a couple of days a month, we screw each other into a coma, and then I head back to NOLA, smug in the knowledge I've got one over on the boss?" He shook his head. "That's not how I want to live my life. Enjoying scraps and sneaking around."

"Well, you won't have to sneak around. You won't have to do anything."

"Fine, Addy. Just fucking fine." He grabbed his jeans and stabbed his feet into the legs. "You don't want to fight for this, then there's not much point to continuing this conversation."

He would fight but only if she wanted it as much as he did. And apparently, she didn't. *Shit. Done before we're even started.*

He'd had enough of one-sided relationships to last a lifetime.

13

ONE WEEK of sleepless nights later, Harper poured a generous glass of Merlot, set it on the kitchen island, and nudged it toward Addison.

"I need to stop drinking," Addison lied.

"Uh-huh." Harper took a healthy gulp of her own.

"So, any news on the team owners' grapevine?"

Harper lifted one petite shoulder. "Thought you didn't want to know."

"Don't be a smart-ass," Addison snapped, and then immediately regretted her testiness. "Sorry. It's just—I'm worried he's screwed up his career over a piece of tail."

"A mighty fine piece of tail."

Addison tried to look annoyed. "Guilty. I do have a great ass but it's only supposed to get *me* into trouble. And while I hate what he did, I still want the best for him."

"What if the best is for him is to be with you?"

"He could have had me. A few times a year. Now he has nothing, the idiot."

Ford had to ruin it by going rogue. He didn't want snatches of paradise here and there like an ordinary horndog. Oh, no. This guy claimed his actions came from the heart, but how could he know after such a short time? And how was it any different than with Michael, who had practically mail-ordered her out of a Victoria's Secret catalog? All her life, she'd been judged on her looks. She couldn't trust that Ford had fallen so quickly based on such a short acquaintance.

You mean, like you did, Addison?

That was different. Who wouldn't fall for a guy like Ford —hot, funny, more evolved than average, and mature beyond his years? She'd called him a boy. There was nothing *boy* about Ford Callaghan. She knew he was looking to remake his life, reconnect with his family, get honest and serious about it to the level he was about his job. It just so happened that in doing that he'd impacted his career.

And all because of her.

His final words, the words she'd played over and over again, came back to her. *You don't want to fight for this, then there's not much point to continuing this conversation.* The problem was, she wasn't sure she had it in her to fight again. Even if she did love him.

But she could still be concerned for him. As a friend. "Back to my original question. Have you heard anything about Michael's plans for Ford?"

Harper pursed her lips. "Not specifically, but he'll make his life hell. It's what I'd do."

"God, you should have been born with balls."

Her friend gave an evil grin. "That's what my father constantly tells me. At least he used to." A shadow crossed her face at the mention of the man who had wanted sons but was saddled with daughters he couldn't appreciate. Henry the VIII had nothing on Clifford Chase.

Harper seemed to give herself an inward shake. "I know you miss Callaghan."

She didn't deny it. "Not quite enough to get over his me-the-man behavior."

"I dunno. There's something very romantic about a guy putting his woman before his career. I know he should have discussed it with you first, but it was actually kind of noble and old-fashioned. He wasn't asking Michael's permission. He was adhering to bro code by giving his boss a heads-up and, at the same time, making his intentions toward you clear. And yes, he called you out because maybe you needed that push. You wanna shit or get off the pot?"

"Bro code? Shit or get off the pot? You've been spending far too long with those meatheads in the locker room. I mean, would you date a hockey player?"

Harper looked uncomfortable again. Twice in as many minutes, and not like her at all.

"Hey, have you actually dated one and didn't tell me?"

Her friend blanched. Addison had evidently hit a sore spot.

"Bad experience?"

"Ancient history." She took another pull of her wine, a longer one this time. So odd, Addison had never seen Harper look so . . . un-Harper.

Addison reached out and squeezed her friend's hand. "You're always listening to my problems. Please know I'm here for you if you ever want to download. Like a good bra. Supportive. Lifts you up. Always close to your heart."

Harper smiled, though it took a couple seconds longer than usual for that sun to reach her eyes.

"My father told me not to get involved with any of the hockey players, not if I wanted to be taken seriously in this business. But I thought I knew better and . . . well, let's just say this guy I chose wasn't very nice to me. After that experience, I realized my father was right. I'd never get any respect from the players if I was in a personal relationship with one. The classic management-labor divide, made doubly difficult when the manager is a woman."

She brightened, having worked to haul herself out of a difficult memory. "But Ford is one of the good ones. Because I've never once seen a guy—any guy—put what supposedly means the most to him on the line for a woman."

"Except the Chicago mayor—what's his name again? The guy who tanked the election last year to prove he loved the firefighter."

"Eli Cooper. And Alexandra Dempsey-Cooper is a very lucky woman. Okay, so Ford's stunt is up there with that move. But do you appreciate it? Oh, no. All you can see is the fact he didn't run it by you first."

Addison pointed at Harper. "That's important. After Michael, I need someone who sees me as an equal, not as a prize in a fight. That's how I felt with my ex. Like a trophy to go with his magnate status. Nothing else."

Harper looked thoughtful. "Callaghan screwed up, honey. But think about why he did it. The guy is in the prime of his career and look what he risked to win you. What he's still risking because by no means is this over. Michael's not going to let it lie."

True, he wouldn't. That lump in Addison's gut turned heavier.

Harper studied her. "I feel like there's more here. Yeah, it wasn't Callaghan's finest moment but can't you see beyond that to the layer that lies beneath? The guy's nuts about you."

That feeling of discomfort about not having anything to offer beyond her looks prickled her skin. She knew she was smart and driven and kind. But she had a hard time seeing herself through Ford Callaghan's rose-colored sex goggles.

She rubbed along her collarbone, trying to temper her distress. "How could he be so sure? What does he see in me that's any different than what every other guy sees in me?"

"Oh, Addy, honey . . ." Harper shook her head in disbelief. "What did he see the first night he talked to you?"

Addison's cheeks burned in memory. That first night, on the hotel balcony, was like something from an erotic fairy tale. "He didn't see anything. He just heard my voice." They were two perfect strangers joking, laughing, flirting. Connecting.

"Exactly. You didn't know what he looked like, that he was a famous hockey player who had just won the Cup. He had no clue you were Addison Williams, world-renowned model. That anonymity was the ultimate blessing for both of you. He could be himself, just some horny dude. And it was the same for you. All you had to go on was his voice and whatever the hell he said to get your rocks off in the company of a total stranger."

Addison covered her face and peeked through the cage of her fingers. "I shouldn't have told you a thing."

"Hey, I'm living vicariously through your filthy-sexy shenanigans. But don't you see? He didn't know what you looked like or who you were. Based on your voice and some admittedly creepy eavesdropping, he thought you were sexy and funny and smart. And later, he still had no idea who you were or what you looked like, yet he tracked you down because he felt you'd shared something real."

The woman had a point. They *had* shared something real, something impossible to fake. Every moment she'd spent with him since had built on that initial encounter, and she'd loved learning more about him in that week he was in

NOLA. *He's kind. He's invested. In me.* Could she trust there was a future to be found here?

Harper reached over and curled her fingers around Addison's palm. "You asked what he sees in you? He sees Addy, my amazing friend, who is as beautiful inside as she is out."

Addison threw her arms around this tiny powerhouse of a woman, almost crushing her in the process. "Thank you for being here for me."

Harper chuckled against Addison's neck.

"What?"

"Bet he was pretty relieved you turned out to be so damn fine."

FORD CHECKED HIS MAILBOX. Junk, junk, and more junk. What was he expecting? A handwritten invitation back into Addy's life? After she had made it clear she didn't want a relationship, he'd slunk back to New Orleans with his tail between his legs. Though he wondered if he'd be a NOLA resident for much longer.

Babineaux hadn't said a word. Neither had the Rajuns' GM or anyone in the front office. His agent was waiting for a call that said he'd be traded out, but Ford knew better. Babineaux was going to make him suffer, wait out the last day of the contract. Two more years, and he'd be lucky if he got any ice time at all.

He could have withstood it if he had her. So much for trying to be a fucking adult.

He walked into the lobby of the high-rise he'd called home for the last year and nodded at Denny, the doorman.

"Mr. Callaghan, you have a visitor." Denny jerked his

head at the sofa in the reception area, where a big guy with the Callaghan dark eyes and stubborn chin stood.

"Hey," Jackson said, his greeting wary.

"Jax." Ford's heart thumped hard against his rib cage. His brother was here. *Why the hell is my brother here?* "Are the kids okay? Marcy?"

"Yeah, yeah, everyone's fine. I came to talk."

Shit, four words Ford had never expected to hear out of his brother's mouth. He'd have loved to hear some conversation beyond "here, talk to the kids" from the prick in the last ten years, but now wasn't the time for recrimination. Ford had said his piece back in Chicago, got what he thought was the last word. Now Jax had come all the way to NOLA, and Ford was damn sure it wasn't to play the blame game.

"Let's go upstairs."

They took the elevator in silence, but it wasn't awkward. Or not nearly as awkward as the bruising silences of the past. Ford let himself into his apartment and held the door for Jax. His brother looked around—not much to see. After sixteen months, he still had stuff in boxes, no pictures on the wall, only takeout, pop, and creamer in the fridge. He did, however, have photos of Jax, Marcy, and the kids on the mantel, along with a family shot of his parents and Paulie.

"Haven't made yourself at home, then?"

"I'd planned to unpack this summer, but now I'm not sure there's much point."

Jax wouldn't have heard what'd happened with Babineaux, but he was fluent in the language of defeat. "You getting traded out?"

"Hard to say. The org's keeping their cards close to their chest."

Jax frowned, clearly not understanding the entire story but not willing to push. "I was out of line, Ford. Talking about your woman that way. I had no idea it was that serious."

Ford grabbed a couple Cokes from the fridge and passed one to his brother. "Well, it's not. I told her ex I planned to date her, and she dumped me."

"Fuck." Jax sat down, his mouth gaping. "You went to Babineaux and . . . shit, staked your claim? Are you crazy?"

Obviously. No one seemed to be appreciating his effort to sac up here. "I was trying to clear a path for us to be together. Trying to show her I'll do what it takes to make this work. That she doesn't have to worry about it."

"'Cause you took care of it?"

Discomfort chewed at his insides. Acting like Ford-knows-best had seemed like such a brilliant plan. He should have understood that a woman like Addy wouldn't enjoy being dictated to.

Joking about it was easier than admitting he screwed up. "So she's chosen not to see the finer details."

"Women." Jax cocked his head. "Can I call her names now?"

Ford grinned. "Nope. She's still my girl, she just needs to come around to the idea."

"Jesus, you were always so stubborn. Practice would be over, and you'd still be out there running drills because you had to get it perfect."

"Had to keep up with the two of you."

"We didn't make it easy on ya, kid." Jax took a slug of his Coke and then a breath that even Ford could hear shuddering. *Ah, shit, here it comes.* "I fucked up, Fordie. That night. Every night after. Yeah, Paulie was the one celebrating, but I should have stayed sober to look after you both."

Ford shook his head. "This isn't about us switching up the blame, bro. Mistakes were made, and I'm not asking for

In Skates Trouble　　123

you to step up and take that burden on. Christ knows we've both suffered, even more because we couldn't weather this together. I've fuckin' missed you, is all."

Jax took another draft because hell, that was pretty heavy. "I've missed you, too. I've missed pushing you around. And I've missed the game."

"So. You've missed violence and hockey."

Jax's mouth stretched into the smile Ford had missed with a raw ache. "Inseparable. And I did list you first."

They laughed at that, probably louder than it deserved, but they needed to reset, and an overdone guffaw was as good as any. Neither of them were huggers or talkers, after all.

Ford's phone rang, which was perfect timing. Getting a touch sugary there.

It was his agent. "Gotta take this."

Five minutes later, he emerged from the bedroom, not quite believing what he'd heard. Jax was finishing up a phone call and by the low murmurs, it sounded like it was Marcy.

"You fill her in?"

Jax nodded. "She's relieved we're on the same wavelength again. And she wants me to get her some beignets."

Priorities, Marcy had 'em. "You're staying for a while, though, right?"

"Just one night. All I could swing from work. I hear the food's good in this town."

"Yeah, it is." He thought back to the conversation he'd just had with Tommy. "And I'm gonna need your advice about something. Something big."

14

FORD LAID the pen down on the mahogany table and took another look at the signature, the last one in a stack of papers. He'd finally finished what he'd started when he walked into Michael Babineaux's office less than a month ago. He'd completely fucked his career.

His agent, Tommy, coughed beside him, and Ford raised his gaze to meet the expectant expressions of the suits across the table. Representatives of the Chicago Rebels, second worst team in the league.

And he was now their star right winger.

Clifford Chase, the maverick owner had passed away suddenly ten days ago and his daughter Harper was sitting in on the signing, along with Brian Rennie, the Rebels' General Manager, and Kenneth Bailey, the team's lawyer.

The lawyer quickly snatched the signed contracts from under Ford's nose, probably worried buyer's remorse would kick in and Ford would decide tearing up those legal documents was better than saddling himself with a losing team. The Rebels now had a world-class, Cup-winning player. Apparently saner minds had prevailed, largely down to his agent playing tough and earning his ten percent. Ford wasn't quite sure how Tommy had pulled it off, but it was a decent deal, all considered.

He'd be lying if he said the chance to be in the same city as Addison didn't enter the equation as well.

The suits rose, everyone shook hands, and they all headed for the exit, the mood somber because the organization had recently lost one of their own.

"Ford, could you wait a moment?" Harper asked.

Ford nodded his okay at Tommy who shot him a look of *no more career-changing heart-to-hearts with management, please.* Alone with Harper, Ford turned around to find her eyeing him speculatively.

"Sorry about your father, Harper."

She nodded, though he'd venture to say she didn't look overly upset. Her contentious relationship with Chase was well-known in the league.

She leaned against the table. "Welcome to the team?"

"You know why I did it."

She smiled regally. "Yeah, I know. What I also know is you had choices and the Rebels would be considered the last team you should have gone for. *But* let's not forget that you did put this ride in motion all by yourself. What the hell did you think was going to happen? That Michael would give his blessing to the young stud putting it to his ex-wife?"

"I thought we could be adults about it," he said for the fiftieth fucking time.

She shook her head. "That's pretty cute, Callaghan. No wonder Addy fell for you."

Fell for him? Maybe, for a moment in time. But she picked herself right back up pretty quickly. Dusted herself off even quicker.

"How is she?"

"Oh, fine. Busy settling into her new place, kicking satin-covered ass." Hard as nails, this woman betrayed nothing in those green eyes of hers. "I think you're going to find Chicago much better suited to your particular style, Killer. We like people who leave it all out there on the ice. People who give one-hundred-fifty percent, and play with their hearts as well as their sticks. I need that this year. I need you."

Heart was not the problem. He'd always led with it—though Jax would call this decision dick-led all the way—and his dumb heart-dick pumped blood through the veins of a born-to-score hockey player. He'd make the best of it because that's what he had always done.

She looked at her phone. "Now would you mind waiting here a second? I need to grab something for you."

"Sure."

She click-clacked out, all five-feet nothing of her. Ford had wondered how a woman would fare in the cutthroat world of hockey. It looked like he might have underestimated Harper Chase.

"Ford?"

He whipped around at the sound of a new voice. *Her* voice, the one that seduced him in the dark all those weeks ago and still had the power to make him lose his mind.

She was here. His Addy.

"Got a minute?"

Did he. He had his whole life ahead of him, and at least the next two years of it in Chicago.

The month since he'd seen her last had only made her more sublime, but she also looked nervous, which was strange on her. This woman had strutted down catwalks, bared her beautiful body to the world, and for some reason she was nervous.

In Skates Trouble

"How've you been?" he asked because even though he wanted to get to the good—or bad—stuff, he needed more time to enjoy the novelty of seeing her a little longer.

"I wanted to apologize for what happened a couple of weeks ago. I said some things I shouldn't have."

"No, sweetheart, I should be apologizing. I pretty much decided that I was going to out a relationship we'd barely scratched the surface of. Addy, I don't regret staking my claim, but I do regret how I went about it. I've spent years being dishonest with myself and holding in my feelings instead of having it out with my family. I didn't want that for us. I wanted us to start off on the right foot." He shook his head. "And then I go and put that foot in my mouth."

"I know you meant well but for the last eighteen months I've been trying to live life on my own terms, without falling under the thumb of a man. I'm done with all of that. I make my own decisions."

Ah, fuck. So she'd just come here to ream him out on being an overbearing alpha dick. Fair enough.

"I hear you, Addy. I thought—hell, I thought I was being all mature about it."

"Michael doesn't do mature."

"Yeah, I'm getting that."

Anger flitted across her face and she started pacing. "You completely risked screwing your career, Ford. Even Harper said so. And then Michael confirmed he wanted to destroy you when I talked to him."

His heart jerked. "You talked to him?"

She stopped treading a rut in the carpet. "Of course I did. And I may have . . ." She hesitated and he took a few steps toward her.

"You may have what?"

"I may have persuaded him to trade you."

Ford did not like the sound of that. "Persuaded him? How, Addy?"

"Let's just say that Michael is not as squeaky clean as he likes to present. Nothing too shady, but I exercised marital privilege 101 and told him if he couldn't be an adult about it and play you, then he needed to trade you to the best team that offered for you. But not for one second did I think the Rebels were in with a chance. You were supposed to go to a decent team, Ford. Like Philly or New York."

Tommy had been surprised at the range of offers, too, though his agent had definitely taken a lot more credit for this than the little prick deserved. *Babineaux wants to see the back of you, and he's willing to give you to a top-shelf team.* Then thirty seconds later, *you're going where?*

"I chose Chicago. I chose the Rebels."

She faced him, vulnerability in the set of her chin. Hesitancy ruled her expression, doubt that she might not receive a good reception when he'd been aching for her forever.

"My family's here, so it's not a terrible move. Those two years would be time well spent reconnecting with my brother and making sure my nephews don't pick up any bad habits on the ice."

"How are things with Jackson?"

"We talked." He felt a grin tugging at his lips at the memory. "Well, he came to see me in New Orleans and we grunted companionably. All good, and it'll only get better now that I'm here."

Her nod was slow, her swallow audible. "I'm glad there's a silver lining."

"I'd say there's probably more than that, Addy."

Her gaze snapped to his. "There is?"

"I'd have thought there's a lace-trimmed pair of designer panties waiting at the end of this rainbow."

In Skates Trouble 129

A smile teased the corner of her mouth. "Is rainbow your dick in this euphemism?"

"No. It's the brightness after the storm. I might have hoped that once I was here we could start over. You and me."

"Ford." Her voice was filled with wonder, her eyes welling with emotion. "Did you really turn down other teams to give us a shot?"

He did, but at its heart, there had been no choice. And there was something about the underdog nature of working with the Rebels that appealed to him. The Rajuns had their Cinderella run last year—maybe he could bring some of that magic to the second worst franchise in the league. Coupled with his family situation and the prospect of a relationship with a woman like Addy, it made for an adventure he was happy to ride out.

"There you go again," she said, swiping at her eyes, "making another decision without consulting me. I used the dirt I had on my ex to undo the damage you had done and you go ahead and ruin it . . ."

"Addy, don't cry. My heart shrivels to nothing when you cry." He pulled her into his arms, the only way he could think to bring his heart back to life. She fit just right, but then she had from the start. That voice of hers, that strength of character, the missing puzzle piece in his life.

"That's twice now, you idiot," she said, sniffling. "Twice you've screwed yourself. You suck at winning, Ford Callaghan."

"Good thing I'm amazing in the sack." He cupped her neck, using his thumb to wipe away her tears. Her bottom lip was like a perfect little pillow, and he ghosted a soft finger pad over it, loving this feeling of closeness. Of holding her against him and comforting her as she'd done for him so many times already.

"I love that you did that for me," he murmured against her soft hair. "I love that you approached this man you could probably do without seeing or talking to ever again and went to bat for me. And I'm sorry I ruined your plan to land me in another city, far away from the woman I'm crazy about. But, you see, I think I knew I was sealing my fate the minute I walked into his office. I think a part of me had already decided that making the ultimate play for the woman of my dreams was how I wanted to be remembered."

Winning Addy was how he wanted to be remembered.

"You're not sorry at all."

"Hard to be sorry when I'm holding you close enough to feel your heart beating in tune with mine." He wandered his hand to the beautiful curve of her ass and pulled her close. "Now, we're going to date, Addison Williams."

"Okay."

"Dinners, movies, the works. Out in the open, no more hiding in the shadows. I'm proud you're mine, and I want everyone to know."

Her teary smile felled him. Dead, keeled over, not getting up.

"I think I'm going to enjoy having a hot stud-trophy on my arm, Callaghan. A boy toy who makes me look good."

He'd happily take on that job. Every skill on his résumé was designed with pleasing her in mind.

"I was born to make you look good, Addy. Now how about you welcome me to Chicago properly?"

She sniffed again, but this time he heard humor and acceptance in it. "What did you have in mind?"

"Give me your mouth, sweetheart."

And then she kissed him like he was oxygen and she was

In Skates Trouble

131

dying to breathe, and he knew, God he knew, that he was in the right place at last. With the right woman and a future he couldn't wait to begin.

When he let her up for air, he whispered, "I reckon your ex did me a massive favor."

She smiled against his mouth. "Oh, yeah?"

"The guy might have dumped me with the second-worst team in the league, but he landed me in the same city as the hottest woman on the planet."

She laughed. "Praise my ex."

"Praise your freakin' ex."

EPILOGUE

Two months later ...

ADDISON CHECKED her reflection in the streaky mirror behind the bar at Jimmy's Tap. Good enough. While she recognized she still had an image to maintain as the face and body of *Beautiful* by Addison, it was a relief not to be so beholden to other people's expectations of her. The only person she needed to stay sexy for was the man walking into the bar this very moment.

"Surprise!" A roar went up from the crowd on seeing Ford, star right winger for the Chicago Rebels. He turned to Jax beside him with a look of *what the fuck* before breaking out into that big, goofy smile she loved. The birthday boy—twenty-seven years old today—shook hands and accepted back pats on his stride to where she leaned against the bar.

"Happy birthday, Callaghan," she said, throwing her arms around him.

Molding herself to his solidity was both grounding and exhilarating. For a boy toy six years younger than her old bones—though Ford liked to insist it was closer to five and a half—he was definitely the mature one in this relationship.

"You have anything to do with this, Bright Eyes?"

She shrugged. "I might have. And your sister-in-law is a force to be reckoned with."

"Needs to be, married to a Callaghan."

The last two months had been amazing with Ford at her side and in her bed. The Rebels' season had gotten off to a rocky start but Harper was taking charge with new acquisitions, one of whom had just walked up to them.

"DuPre," Ford said, smiling at Remy DuPre, the latest addition to the Rebels' offense. Dubbed "the Unluckiest Guy in the League" because of how close he'd come to the Cup with no cigar, the Louisiana native cut a compellingly rugged figure with his lived-in face, broad shoulders, and a frame more suited to a linebacker.

Not that she had eyes for anyone but Ford. Still, Remy had undeniable ice-appeal.

Ford shook hands with Remy. "Have you met my Addy?" The pride in his voice melted Addison's knees. *My Addy.* And oh how she was. Completely, without question.

Remy shook Addison's hand. "Ain't had the pleasure, *chérie.*" He raised it and kissed her knuckles, adding a cheeky wink.

Addison laughed. "Oh, it's all true, then."

"What is?"

"That Southern charm that gets the ladies warm." She drew her hand back and fanned her face. "My, my, Mr. DuPre, have pity on my sensibilities."

"No quarter given, not where a pretty lady is concerned."

"Told ya he was trouble," Ford said easily, with no machismo or jealousy. She loved how sure he was of himself and of her love for him. So different from Michael.

"Oh, babe, there's Harper. I'll be back in a second." Leaving him with the kind of kiss that would keep his desire burning in her absence, Addison moved off toward the bar's entrance, but not before she heard Remy ask Ford how he managed to land a quality woman like Addison.

Ford's response followed in her wake and hugged her heart. "I ask myself that question every fuckin' day. She's something, isn't she?"

Damn straight, she was something.

Addison reached Harper who had just parted ways with her "date" for the evening, Kenneth Bailey. Valiantly and ever useful, he tried cutting a path through the mass of ice-honed muscle to get Harper a drink at the bar.

After a brief hug, Addison stated with not a little coyness, "So. Kenneth."

"What about him?"

Addison raised an eyebrow, though she had nothing on Harper's favorite method of communication.

"Don't give me that eyebrow of disapproval, Addy Williams. I practically dislocated mine when you hooked up with Callaghan."

"Which is why I'm being a good friend now. I know you're not sleeping with him. And I can't believe he's still hanging on your arm."

"So men only stick around if the dangling carrot of sex is in play?"

Addy cocked a hip. "You've had him on a string for a year, Harper."

"Kenneth knows the score. I've told him I'm not interested in a relationship right now, and we're happy to be each other's plus-one for various events. No expectations, no complications."

No chemistry, thought Addison. She knew her friend had

had a rough time of it lately with her father passing away suddenly and finding herself in the unexpected position of jointly running the team with her two half-sisters, neither of whom she got along with all that well. Three bickering women attempting to steer a professional sports team to success? The media was having a field day, especially as the jokes wrote themselves.

"So what did you get Ford for his birthday?" Harper asked. "Lemme guess? Anal?"

Addison blushed. Sometimes Harper was really too much.

"Knew it."

"*Nooo.* I haven't given him his gift yet." Her hand flew to her tummy, thinking about how that "gifting" conversation would go. Eager for a rapid subject change, she added, "Your savior's a real charmer, by the way."

"My sav—oh, right." Her gaze tracked to where Ford stood with Remy, darkening on spying the big Cajun with his back to them both. It lingered somewhat longingly on the man's very fine ass. What was it about hockey players and their most excellent butt musculature? As his boss, Harper couldn't get involved with him or even have a little fun, which was a damn shame because if there was one thing Harper needed, it was a little—or a lot of—fun.

"I wonder why he's not married," Addison mused, because she suspected Remy DuPre gave new meaning to "fun." "Or in a relationship."

"Some men aren't cut out for it. You probably found the last magical unicorn in the league."

Warming up, Addison poked the bear a touch. "He's had girlfriends. Plenty of girlfriends."

Annoyance flirted with Harper's usually ice-cool expression. *There it is.* A forbidden romance might be just the ticket . . . Look at how it had worked for Addison.

"Sweetheart, I missed you."

She turned in time to see her man—the man of the night and all her future nights—leaning in for a kiss that made her heart flutter.

On separating, she found Harper and Remy shooting daggers at each other, and she missed the opening salvo because Ford dragged her away. Spoilsport.

"Callaghan," she whined, "I'm trying to stir things up here."

"You need to be stirring things up over here." He pulled her behind a pillar, away from the crowd. "Time for a Ford-Addy check-in."

"Oh, yeah? How're we doing?"

He checked in with her lips, then along the curve of her neck to that sensitive spot along her collarbone. Then his hard body decided to get in on the check-in act as he covered her completely.

"All good." And then, in a reverent, awe-struck tone, "Christ, woman, I love you."

Her heart did a funny spin. She felt his love in every lusty kiss and genuine moment they'd spent together since he signed with the Rebels, but he'd not expressed their connection in words. She'd been a little worried that he might feel obliged to say that when she told him her news. To hear him offer it so freely was a gift in itself.

He lifted his head from where he'd been nuzzling gently. "What, nothing? Not even a cheeky 'I know'? Because you have to know how crazy I am about you. How I fell in love with your voice and wit and charm on that balcony."

She tried to remain grave, though joy was bubbling like lava below the surface. "So, you like me for my personality?"

In Skates Trouble 137

"Well, you don't have much else going for you, Bright Eyes." He sighed. "Okay, you're not so bad to look at, I suppose, but I'm not the shallow type who's swayed by a pretty face and a bangin' body." He rolled his hips against her, hitting that sizzling juncture between her thighs just right. "I'm mostly interested in a woman I can talk, argue, and grow old with." Another rub of his erection against her core. Oh, God, they needed to find somewhere, anywhere, *now*. "Soul-deep. That's the connection I want."

His mouth captured hers, avowing that profound, ever-deepening connection, one that had sparked on a hot summer night in the shadows. One that had blossomed in the light into something so all-consuming she refused to imagine her life without it.

She'd fallen in love with a man who risked it all to stoke the embers of desire created that first night and turn those sparks into flames of love. Who saw what she couldn't because her heart was closed to the possibilities. Who respected and cherished all she was.

Ford "Killer" Callaghan slayed her every time, and she was happy to die in his arms every night.

"I love you, too, Callaghan," she whispered. She brought his wandering hand from her ass to her stomach. "Happy birthday, Daddy-to-be."

Any doubts she had that he might not be thrilled at this news faded as his face transformed from desire to shock to unadulterated joy. Radiant happiness shimmered in his chocolate-drop eyes, ones she hoped their baby would inherit.

"Looks like we'll be slipping away to Jimmy's office very soon."

She sighed dramatically, then added with a grin, "If we must."

ACKNOWLEDGMENTS

Thanks to Marion Archer for her stellar editing, Karen Lawson for her attention to detail during copyediting, and Sweet n' Spicy Designs for my awesome cover.

THE CHICAGO REBELS

Three estranged sisters inherit their late father's failing hockey franchise and are forced to confront a man's world, their family's demons, and the battle-hardened ice warriors skating into their hearts.

~

Irresistible You (Chicago Rebels, #1)

Harper Chase has just become the most powerful woman in the NHL after the death of her father Clifford Chase, maverick owner of the Chicago Rebels. But the team is a hot mess—underfunded, overweight, and close to tapping out of the league. Hell-bent on turning the luckless franchise around, Harper won't let anything stand in her way. Not her gender, not her sisters, and especially not a veteran player with an attitude problem and a smoldering gaze designed to melt her ice-compacted defenses.

Veteran center Remy "Jinx" DuPre is on the downside of

a career that's seen him win big sponsorships, fans' hearts, and more than a few notches on his stick. Only one goal has eluded him: the Stanley Cup. Sure, he's been labeled as the unluckiest guy in the league, but with his recent streak of good play, he knows this is his year. So why the hell is he being shunted off to a failing hockey franchise run by a ball-buster in heels? And is she seriously expecting him to lead her band of misfit losers to a coveted spot in the playoffs?

He'd have a better chance of leading Harper on a merry skate to his bed...

∾

So Over You (Chicago Rebels, #2)

Isobel Chase knows hockey. She played NCAA, won Olympic silver, and made it thirty-seven minutes into the new National Women's Hockey League before an injury sidelined her dreams. Those who can't, coach, and a position as a skating consultant to her late father's hockey franchise, the Chicago Rebels, seems like a perfect fit. Until she's assigned her first job: the man who skated into her heart as a teen and relieved her of her pesky virginity. These days, left-winger Vadim Petrov is known as the Czar of Pleasure, a magnet for puck bunnies and the tabloids alike. But back then . . . let's just say his inability to sink the puck left Isobel frustratingly scoreless.

Vadim has a first name that means "ruler," and it doesn't stop at his birth certificate. He dominates on the ice, the practice rink, and in the backseat of a limo. But a knee injury has produced a bad year, and bad years in the NHL don't go unrewarded. His penance? To be traded to a troubled team where his personal coach is Isobel Chase, the woman who drove him wild years ago when they were hormonal teens. But apparently the feeling was not entirely mutual.

That Vadim might have failed to give Isobel the pleasure that was her right is intolerable, and he plans to make it up to her—one bone-melting orgasm at a time. After all, no player can perfect his game without a helluva lot of practice ...

∼

Undone by You (Chicago Rebels, #3)

Dante Moretti has just landed his dream job: GM of the Chicago Rebels. And screw the haters who think there should be an asterisk next to his name because he's the first out managing executive in pro hockey. He's earned the right to be here and nothing will topple him off that perch—especially not an incredibly inconvenient attraction to his star defenseman, Cade "Alamo" Burnett. Cade has always been careful to keep his own desires on the down low, but his hot Italian boss proves to be a temptation he can't resist. Sure, they both have so much to lose, but no one need ever know...

As Dante and Cade's taboo affair heats up off the ice and their relationship gets more and more intense, they'll have to decide: is love worth risking their careers? Or is this romance destined to be forever benched?

∼

Hooked on You (Chicago Rebels, #4)

Violet Vasquez never met her biological father, so learning he left his beloved hockey franchise—the Chicago Rebels—to her is, well, unexpected. Flat broke and close to homeless, Violet is determined to make the most of this sudden opportunity. Except dear old dad set conditions that require she takes part in actually running the team with the half-sisters she barely knows. Working with these two strangers and overseeing a band of hockey-playing lugs is not on her agenda...until she lays eyes on the Rebels captain and knows she has to have him.

Bren St. James has been labeled a lot of things: the Puck Prince, Lord of the Ice, Hell's Highlander...but it's the latest tag that's making headlines: *washed-up alcoholic has-been.* This season, getting his life back on track and winning the Cup are his only goals. With no time for relationships—except the fractured ones he needs to rebuild with his beautiful daughters—he's finding it increasingly hard to ignore sexy, all-up-in-his-beard Violet Vasquez. And when he finds himself in need of a nanny just as the playoffs are starting, he's faced with a temptation he could so easily get hooked on.

For two lost souls, there's more on the line than just making the best of a bad situation... there might also be a shot at the biggest prize of all: love.

Wrapped Up in You (Chicago Rebels, #4.5)

The holidays are coming and hockey player, Cade "Alamo" Burnett knows exactly what he wants for Christmas: an assurance that his happily-ever-after with Chicago Rebels general manager, Dante Moretti, stays that way. But festive gremlins are conspiring to throw a wrench in the forever Cade and Dante fought so hard for. With their personal and professional lives clashing, can they find their way back to each other—or are they destined to find coal in their stockings come Christmas morning?

ABOUT THE AUTHOR

Originally from Ireland, *USA Today* bestselling author Kate Meader cut her romance reader teeth on Maeve Binchy and Jilly Cooper novels, with some Harlequins thrown in for variety. Give her tales about brooding mill owners, over-sexed equestrians, and men who can rock an apron, a fire hose, or a hockey stick, and she's there. Now based in Chicago, she writes sexy contemporary romance with big-hearted guys and strong heroines - and heroes - who can match their men quip for quip.

~

www.katemeader.com

ALSO BY KATE MEADER

Rookie Rebels

GOOD GUY

INSTACRUSH

MAN DOWN

Chicago Rebels

IRRESISTIBLE YOU

SO OVER YOU

UNDONE BY YOU

HOOKED ON YOU

WRAPPED UP IN YOU

Laws of Attraction

DOWN WITH LOVE

ILLEGALLY YOURS

THEN CAME YOU

Hot in Chicago

REKINDLE THE FLAME

FLIRTING WITH FIRE

MELTING POINT

PLAYING WITH FIRE

SPARKING THE FIRE

FOREVER IN FIRE

COMING IN HOT

Tall, Dark, and Texan
EVEN THE SCORE
TAKING THE SCORE
ONE WEEK TO SCORE

Hot in the Kitchen
FEEL THE HEAT
ALL FIRED UP
HOT AND BOTHERED

Made in the USA
Columbia, SC
20 June 2020